"We must change the system, in order to reflect our better selves."

President of the United States
State of the Union
January 12, 2016

2016

What they have said about the Vice Presidency...

"The most insignificant office that ever the invention of man contrived."

John Adams

"I do not propose to be buried until I am dead."

Daniel Webster

"I go to funerals. I go to earthquakes.

Nelson Rockefeller

"The man with the best job in the country is the Vice President. All he has to do is get up every morning and ask, 'How is the President?'"

Will Rogers

"Democracy means that anyone can grow up to be President, and anyone who doesn't can grow up to be Vice President."

Johnny Carson

"Once there were two brothers… one ran away to sea, the other was elected Vice President, and nothing was heard from either of them again."

Thomas Marshall

"The Vice Presidency is not worth a bucket of warm spit."

John Nance Garner

The VeeP

Ned Schwartz

This is a book published by para*Flix*®

© 2016 by para*Flix*®

All rights reserved under International and Pan-American Copyright conventions. Published in the United States by para*Flix*®

Port St. Lucie

With para*Flix*... It's OK to hear voices! ®and para*Flix* are a registered trademarks of para*Flix*®

www.para*Flix*.com

ASIN: B017WMM0X8

ISBN: 13-978-0-9972303-0-7

For all the students I had the honor of learning from...
with thanks.

Remember... it depends!

CONTENTS

SUMMARY

A political docu-drama blueprint on how to become Vice President of the United States... without all the usual distractions like debates, primaries, fundraising, Super PACs, or even worrying about the outcome of the 2016 election, by running as a bi-partisan candidate for both parties.

Follow Eli Eaton, a successful restaurant owner as he embarks on a journey to elevate the office of the VPOTUS into a position worthy of the second highest elected office in our country. If you are fed up with all the partisan gridlock and all the political histrionics of both parties and the Presidential candidates, then see what Eli Eaton has up his sleeve.

The VeeP shows how the people can have a voice in who is nominated to become our next Vice President and what his/her responsibilities should be, by employing Eli's two simple formulae for resolving conflict and finding happiness in life... **Q=R≥E** and his 760° method for employing fresh and unique points of view for finding solutions to life's challenges.

Experience Eli's journey with an innovative way to read... with para*Flix*®... a hybrid movie script/novel designed as a quick one or two night read, that flows like a novel, but formatted like a script. You get to be the producer! Cast all the roles with your favorite actors [dead or alive], or you and your friends as the stars... and imagine their voices as you read the dialog and imagine the scenes playing out in your mind's eye with the cast you choose, while enjoying a totally new role playing reading experience.

Before reading *The VeeP*...

You may want to experience a whole new way to read.

Would you like to make *The VeeP* into a motion picture as you read it? Go ahead... you're the Producer!

Read the brief description of each starring character at the end of the book, and then cast the roles with actors [dead or alive] you wish to play these roles, or cast your friends, or yourself in the starring roles... in order to bring *The VeeP* to life... for your own personal movie production... and hear their voices while you read and imagine the scenes while you experience this...

para*Flix*® DocuDrama

It's a new kind of book.

With **para*Flix***... It's OK to hear voices!®

The VeeP

FADE IN:

ON SCREEN:

COPY OF THE U.S. CONSTITUTION...

TYPED ON SCREEN UNDER:

"One person can't make a difference."

"You can't fight city hall."

"Nothing ever gets done in Washington."

1. The Seed

FADE IN:
UNIVERSITY CAMPUS:

ON SCREEN:

26 YEARS AGO...

CUT TO:
CLASS ROOM:

SHOT IN BLACK AND WHITE
SLIGHT BLUR... IN THE PAST:

POLITICAL SCIENCE 101:

[view of 20 students sitting with professor in front, on the last day of class, reviewing for the upcoming final paper assignment...]

PROFESSOR DIETRICH

... so in summary, remember the two most important concepts we explored this semester... first, in order to satisfy any constituent's happiness, and achieve political success for yourself, merely apply the formula we've been using all semester, [Q]uality, or happiness occurs when [R]eality equals or exceeds [E]xpectatons... **Q=R≥E** and second, the 760° method for finding fresh and unique solutions to solving life's challenges.

It's your responsibility to establish appropriate expectations through your communication with your constituents, that means, **ASK QUESTIONS, DON'T LIE AND DON'T OVER PROMISE...** then you need to mobilize any available resources, namely money, people and ideas... to create the best possible reality given whatever budget and/or human resource constraints there may be... and it doesn't matter if we're talking about local government or the federal government. The only difference is a few zero's and a couple commas... the process is the same. Period.

And when trying to solve what appear to be unsolvable challenges, first look at the problem from the inside out, looking at all 360°s, then step outside the circle and look again at the problem from the outside, looking in... again using all 360°s, but from the other persons' point of view.

[the professor then writes on the chalkboard:]

"Poli Sci 101 Final Paper Assignment... then he/she writes underneath:

"How can I make a difference?"]

CLASS
Mumbling, moans.

PROFESSOR DIETRICH
This will be due next Friday, 20 pages long... *[class groans]* double spaced, standard margins and citations... *[more class groans]* hey, that's only 250 words a page, a mere collection of the most meaningful 5,000 mono and polysyllabic words you can create. *[more class groans.]* Hey Toto.. you're not in high school anymore... besides, you've got the easy part... I have to read all 100,000 of your words, so make them memorable. Any questions?

STUDENT
Is this supposed to be for society, or for like... me, personally?

PROFESSOR DIETRICH
Yes... any more questions?

CLASS
Moans, grumbling.

PROFESSOR DIETRICH
OK everyone, I'll see you next week, my office.

2. The Big Apple

SLOW FADE IN:
NEW YORK CITY / MANHATTAN:
ON SCREEN:

SUNDAY JULY 10, 2016

[a warm and sunny morning, the bustle of the city is afoot with the din of traffic and summer tourists moving and crowding around a pedestrian area, at 6th Ave and 48th St.]

CUT TO EXTERIOR:

STUDIO BUILDING:

[sounds of outdoor din of crowd fades to sounds of hectic production assistants in a TV studio preparing for the Sunday morning news program, Face the Press, hosted by Mike Rudd.]

CUT TO:

GREEN ROOM:

[Eli Eaton sits off to the side in one corner as former Gov. Ann Barrett, Republican candidate for President with a small entourage including Russ, her campaign manager, Emily Morris, a documentary producer and Dave, the cameraman, and her assigned Secret Service agent come storming in trying to take over the entire room. Production assistants are moving in and out with clipboards and headphones, giving and receiving directions and schedules... all bumping into one another.]

RUSS

Governor, have a seat over there and settle in... I'll go check on things.

ANN

Someone... get me a cup of coffee, cream, two sugars ... and find out exactly what questions I'll be asked! I don't want to look like a high school cheerleader waiting to get banged by the football team.

[whispering to a nodding Dave.]

EMILY
Sounds like she's been there!

ELI

I'm sure in the wake of Newtown, Aurora, Charleston, Oregon and San Bernadino, he's gonna ask how a card carrying NRA member feels about gun control after having her husband murdered in a convenience store robbery... I'm sorry for your loss... and about tighter homeland security since you were at the Fredericksburg bombing last week. *[Pause]* Seriously, I don't think he's gonna ask you where to get a good latte around here. I trust you're doing well after last Monday, it must've been unnerving. Hi by the way, I'm...

*[pretending not to hear the observation or the unsolicited compassion while she looks in the mirror and plays with her hair. Eli shakes his head... smiling to himself knowing that **his** actions from last Monday, may very well have saved her life.]*

ANN
Emily, let me know before you shoot any footage.

EMILY
Governor, I always do... I want to get you in the studio... I think it will give you credibility with the Face the Press set in the background. Dave, take a couple shots in here, then follow her into the studio.

DAVE
You got it.

FTP ASSISTANT 1
You're gonna have to move your camera out into the hallway... it gets pretty hectic in here.

DAVE
No problem.

*[coming into the room with
headphones and a clipboard.]*

FTP ASSISTANT 2
Governor, Mr. Rudd wants to have you on after Mr. Eaton.
We tape the show in real time, so you'll have to be ready to
move with about two minutes notice during the commercial
break.

RUSS
We'll have the Governor ready.

FTP ASSISTANT 2
Great... Mr. Eaton, why don't we start moving you into the
studio and get you mic'ed up... and someone will be in
shortly to prep Governor Barrett.

*[she stands up and is now, pacing
around the doorway.]*

ANN
How long will the first segment run?

FTP ASSISTANT 2
That's up to Mr. Rudd.

[quietly to Ann, as an aside.]

RUSS
We better get ready...$20 bucks this guy won't last three
minutes.

[leaving the room, in the doorway, Eli accidentally brushes up against Emily, then instinctively touches her upper arm to apologize...she briefly clenches up and looks defensively where he's touching her... but quickly loosens up realizing that she actually likes it, even blushing slightly... Eli rotates around while pulling out his wallet and without missing a beat, hands a $20 bill to Ann, speaking first to Emily, and then to Ann...]

ELI
Sorry... and I'll take that bet.

[Ann looking annoyed takes the bill as if she can't be bothered and hands it to Russ.]

ANN
What does he think I am?... and who in the hell does he think he is?

FTP ASSISTANT 1
Haven't you been following Facebook, You Tube and Twitter?...that's Eli Eaton... he's gone viral!

CUT TO:
FACE THE PRESS SET:

[view of cameras, monitors, set.]

18

[Face the Press theme song starts playing...]

RUDD

This Sunday... after the terrorist bombing last week at the Fredericksburg, Virginia July 4th Festival, a grim reminder of the devastation and senseless killings at Aurora, Newtown, Boston, Charleston, Oregon and San Bernadino that are still weighing heavy on our thoughts. The drums for tighter gun control and for tighter homeland security are now beating together as we approach the November election. Joining us later, former Governor Ann Barrett, Republican candidate for President, who not only lost her husband Donald two years ago in a convenience store robbery involving an illegal handgun... and... who also was campaigning only yards away from the bombing last Monday in Fredericksburg... Gov. Barrett will be sharing her unique perspective on both these topics... but first... a man... who is running a grass roots campaign for national office, whose alertness is being credited with saving an untold number of lives last week at the Fredericksburg bombing... Eli Eaton... and no, it's not what you might expect... this candidate has burst upon the scene from a very non-traditional place... not Congress not a Governorship, but from Facebook, Twitter and You Tube... and after last Monday... he's gone viral.

[Pause]

Welcome, it's Sunday, and time to... Face the Press.

[Face the Press *theme continues music playing in background.*]

ON SCREEN:

JULY 10, 2016

FTP ANNOUNCER [off screen]
From our global news headquarters in New York, it's time to... Face the Press, with Mike Rudd.

RUDD
Good morning, we start off this Sunday...

FADE OUT:

TO FLASHBACK:

3. The Root of All Evil

FLASHBACK:

FADE IN:
ON SCREEN:

TEN MONTHS EARLIER...

[a typical fall new england town hall meeting being held in a high school auditorium:]

[view is from the rear, not showing faces of voters]:

[there are hundreds of people sitting, milling around while two town councilmen are standing in the front with a microphone announcing a proposed Zoning By-Law.]

CLOSE IN ON SPEAKERS AT

PODIUM:

FIRST COUNCILMAN

[*in an official monotone.*]

Next is Warrant number 27, a Zoning By-Law which mandates a minimum number of parking spaces for businesses and sets the required area for ingress and egress for all business and commercial facilities in town, as a matter of public safety. Any comments?

[*there is some quiet audience noise, but no one is stepping up to the microphone to comment on the proposal.*]

FIRST COUNCILMAN
There being no comment on Warrant number 27, all in favor say Aye.

[*a clear majority says aye.*]

FIRST COUNCILMAN
All those opposed say Nay.

[*a smattering of nays.*]

FIRST COUNCILMAN
The chair determines there is a clear majority, Warrant number 27 passes.

[*after a brief pause and paper shuffling and taking on an officious tone.*]

FIRST COUNCILMAN
The final Warrant... number 28, a Zoning By-Law listed in your handout. The purpose of this by-law is to regulate the use of home offices. It requires anyone with an office in a residence, register with the Zoning Board for a special permit to engage in said activity within a residential area, by indicating the nature, scope and type of activity that is going on. I will now open the floor for comment.

[at the audience microphone.]

VOTER 1 [CLAIRE]
Looking at subparagraph b. of Warrant 28, it states that there can be no signs, or other outward manifestation of anything other than a residence, correct?

FIRST COUNCILMAN
That is true.

CLAIRE
And subparagraph d. states that there can be no extraneous noise, light, smell or vibration emanating from the residence... correct?

FIRST COUNCILMAN
That is correct.

CLAIRE
So, if there is absolutely no indication of any outside activity going on in my house, other than a normal residence, why then do we have to register with the town what we do in the privacy of our own home? Sounds draconian.

[much applause in support of Voter 1.]

AUDIENCE
Yeahs.

[from the other audience microphone.]

VOTER 2
Why do I need approval for what goes on in the privacy of my own home, just because I have an office in my house? Good Lord, everyone has a home office these days.

[louder.]

AUDIENCE
Yeahs and applause.

FIRST COUNCILMAN
Because, we need to know what is going on in our residential districts. If you have an office in a residential district, we need to know about it and either approve it with a special permit waiver or deny it, if inappropriate. We can't have people conducting business activities in a residential district.

[louder still.]

AUDIENCE
Boos.

VOTER 3

Hey everyone, hold on a moment...we elected our Councilmen so that they would keep things running smoothly in town. They know better than we do what is necessary to keep our town safe and we need to support them.

VOTER 4

If I have an office in my home and I'm just using my computer, what possible reason do you need to know what I'm doing on my computer?

[getting louder and boisterous.]

AUDIENCE

Me toos.

SECOND COUNCILMAN

Because this is a Zoning By-Law. The town is divided into various zones and if any business type activity goes on in a residential district, there needs to be a variance.

VOTER 5

What's wrong with you people? You're a bunch of cry babies... grow up already. What's the big deal? Just do what they want to keep us safe.

FROM AUDIENCE

Thank you Mary Poppins! This isn't Russia!

VOTER 6 [MR. GUSIK]

Listen, I'm a family law attorney, living on Bellevue. Many times a client thinking about a divorce doesn't want to meet me in my office because they don't want to be seen, so they come over to my house. If my activity is a matter of public record, then my client's privacy has been violated when the car is in the driveway. We need to vote down this Warrant.

SECOND COUNCILMAN

That's precisely why we do need this By-Law. Every additional car that comes into a residential district poses a safety threat to our children.

MR. GUSIK

What's the difference if a friend comes over or a client? It's still just two people talking.

CUT TO:

REAR SHOT OF COUPLE SITTING IN AUDIENCE:

[*audience is getting more and more
vocal.
focus in on backs of a couple,
Voters 7 and 8 in audience:*]

VOTER 7
Wow... these guys don't have a clue.

VOTER 8

Last Sunday during Face the Press... you were yelling at the TV... saying the same thing about Sen. McCain and Joe Biden.

VOTER 7

Most of the time... they don't have a clue either. Seriously, why don't you stand up and say something before we have a riot here? You're the one who makes jewelry in her home.

[*in a playful tone, giving him an elbow
in the side and pointing to the
microphone...*]

VOTER 8

Me? There's nothing I can say that'll do any good. This is politics... one person can't change anything!

VOTER 7

That's not entirely true. This is no different than nuclear fission. Just one neutron fired into a critical mass... and boom. $E=mc^2$... Einstein... brilliant guy.

[*Voter 8 is seen slowly turning her head toward Voter 7 shooting him a long, long look.*]

VOTER 7 [CONT'D]
What? It's true... really, I'm right!

VOTER 8
Would you rather be right... or get lucky tonight?

[*pause, stroking his chin, like he's actually thinking about it.*]

VOTER 7

I thought these kind of conversations didn't start until **AFTER** we get married.

[*in a playful tone nudging him...*]

VOTER 8

Forget Einstein, be a man... if we're going to get married in a couple months, you should be looking out for me... do something manly... go ahead, be a neutron.

[*cell phone keeps vibrating, she looks at it.*]
It's him.

VOTER 7
Just put it on airplane mode.

VOTER 8
I'll take care of it.

VOTER 7
OK, I'll show you how one person **CAN** make a difference...
watch and learn!

*[Voter 7 rises and walks toward the
microphone, Voter 8 starts texting.]*

VIEW STILL FROM THE REAR:

VOTER 7 [ELI]
Gentlemen... everyone... what we have here... is a failure...
to communicate!

*[some chuckling from the audience to
the Cool Hand Luke reference.]*
AUDIENCE
You tell 'em Cool Hand.

ELI [CONT'D]
Seriously... I may not be very good at public speaking... but
boy I sure can listen. I totally hear each of your expectations
here, and now you have to hear each other's... so we can
create a reality here acceptable to all of us. *[Simple
Q=R≥E.]* Mr. Harris, Mr. Scanlon, you've gotta take a deep
breath and listen to what these people are saying... you can't
treat them like children, telling them what they can and
cannot do, especially in the privacy of their own homes.

AUDIENCE
Yeahs! Applause.

[looking at Voter 1.]

ELI [CONT'D]
I'm sorry... and what's your name?

CLAIRE
Claire.

ELI
Claire... and you other people... we can't be turning our houses into Mini-Marts, now can we?

CLAIRE
Of course not.

ELI [CONT'D]
... so what we have here is the need to balance conflicting interests... keeping our residential areas intact without the town telling us what we can and can't do in our own homes. So... Mr. Scanlon, Mr. Gusik... come on over here, you guys... and lets shake hands... geez, they even do that before a boxing match for crying out loud. What do you think... this is Congress? I'd like to think we're better than that. Here's what we need to do... Mr. Harris, if there are no signs, no noise and absolutely nothing going on outside of a house, the town has to be OK with that. And Mr. Gusik, you have to be willing to limit the number of cars and traffic coming over to your house to whatever is normal for social visitors, I don't know... 2, 4, 6... whatever cars per day?

[applause breaks out from the audience.]

[shouted out.]

AUDIENCE
Finally... some common sense! I second that motion.

CUT TO:

PODIUM

[whispering to first councilman,
holding hand over the microphone.]

SECOND COUNCILMAN
Who the hell does this prick think he is? Isn't that Eaton, who runs the restaurant?

[nod from other councilman.]

VOTER
I third that amendment. Let's vote already.

FIRST COUNCILMAN
There being a motion to amend and seconded, all in favor of said amendment, say Aye.

AUDIENCE
Ayes

FIRST COUNCILMAN
All opposed, say Nay.

AUDIENCE
[only a handful.]   Nays.

[visibly annoyed and glaring at Eli.]

FIRST COUNCILMAN
There being a clear majority the amendment passes.

AUDIENCE
Cheering, all rights, finally some sense around here!

[*as a vote is taken and the amended By-Law passes by a huge voice vote margin, both councilmen are clearly annoyed that someone had the audacity to question their authority.*]

[*Voter 7 turns around to return to his seat and we finally see it is Eli Eaton, people are high fiving him, patting him on the back, shaking his hand, giving him the OK sign, saying "way to go, Eli" as he walks toward the back of the auditorium, Voter 8 [Marie] gets up and greets him with a quick hug amidst all the adulation.*]
[*with some playful confidence nodding to Marie as they walk out.*]

ELI

Now **THAT'S** how it's done. Q=R≥E... communicate and mobilize. Simple.

VOTER 9
Eli, I thought there was going to be a riot... thanks.

VOTER 10
Eli, you should run for town councilman... you're a natural.

VOTER 11
Screw that... we need you in Washington!

ELI
Love to... all I'll need is a small campaign contribution... say oh, 2 - 3 million!

[*tongue in cheek, gesturing taking his wallet out.*]

VOTER 11
No problem... I'll write you a check!

CUT TO:

4. It's Nothing Personal

LATER THAN EVENING:

MARIE'S DEN:

[*Eli sitting on sofa flipping between CNN, Fox News and MSNBC while Marie plops down and cuddles up to him.*]

MARIE
The kids are finally in bed.

ELI
Did Zack finish his science report?

MARIE
Oh, he finished, but he refuses to check it and clean up his grammar. You know Zack, Mr. One and Done.

ELI
Well, if he wants to be a pastry chef when he grows up, he'd better learn how to check his work... not a lot of room for error when baking a soufflé.

MARIE
Yeah, it wouldn't hurt to clean up after himself in the kitchen, either. You won't believe where I found flour this morning.

[*responding to the TV.*]
ELI
What an idiot!

MARIE
Why do you watch that stuff... it only aggravates you.

ELI

You need to know what they're saying, especially if you disagree... keeps you honest, on your toes.

MARIE

Hey, what did you want to be... when you were Zack's age?

ELI

Gee, it's funny you should bring that up, especially after tonight.

MARIE

What, the town meeting... you wanted to grow up to be a town councilman?

ELI

Please... Actually, I really don't remember ever wanting to be anything... but everyone kept telling me how I was going to grow up to be President one day... my mother, my teachers, my aunts, uncles... geez, it really got annoying after awhile... I hated everyone telling me what I was going to be, so to mess with them, I'd tell them that I didn't want to be President. I wanted to be... Vice President!

[*laughing under her breath.*]

MARIE
Really?

ELI

There, that's exactly how they responded... I always got this funny little chuckle when I said I wanted to be Vice President. They'd ask me... "Eli, what does the Vice President do?" and I'd say, "I don't know." and they'd say... "Hey, in that case, you'll be perfect for the job!" laughing like it was some big joke. Then all through school and even college, I'd be elected president of this group, president of that organization... man, I thought I was doomed to be President.

[jokingly.]

MARIE

Well, we see how that turned out. Not! Seriously, when did you fall off the track?

[responding to commentator's reporting of Judge Scalia's dissent on a ruling.]

ELI

Geez, it really sounds like Judge Scalia is starting to lose it... hey... aren't you the same guy who brought politics to the Supreme Court when you decided the 2000 election? Amazing. Wow, he used to be sharp as a razor... now... 'applesauce' in a Supreme Court ruling? Whoa.

MARIE

Yeah, everybody's a critic. Seriously, what happened?

[thinking back...]

ELI

Well, I graduated college with a Political Science degree, hell, I even wrote a final paper on how to run a low cost, grass roots campaign to become Vice President.

MARIE

Well, what happened?

[*pondering...*]

ELI

Sex.

[*as she nuzzles up to Eli...*]

MARIE

Sex? OK.

[*with just a hint of sarcasm.*]

ELI

Yeah, I discovered sex... then I got married to have more sex... and after all that sex I had Matt... and well, the rest is history... yeah, sex. Besides, everyone knows that a Poli Sci degree is the best education to own a restaurant! Guess if I really wanted to be President, I should have gotten a degree in Restaurant Management!

MARIE

Aaah, I see. I should have guessed... you're a guy... it's always about sex.

[*as he starts to move his arm up her back.*]

ELI

... and your point?

[playfully pulling his arm down.]

MARIE
Whoa, cowboy... first, before we get married... it's kinda like starting all over... I need to know... what do you want to be when you grow up... this time?

ELI
Well, isn't it pretty obvious?

MARIE
What's that?

ELI
Your husband.

MARIE
Aaaah, so you **DO** understand what the Vice President does!?!

[as they embrace and fall onto the sofa laughing... a text beep is heard.]

FADE OUT:

5. This is No Picnic

CUT TO EXTERIOR:
[*New England Fall view of bright colorful leaves.*]

CUT TO:
PIKNIK*S RESTAURANT:

[*a family restaurant with a picnic decor, red checkered motif with picnic tables, wicker food baskets, etc. It is very busy, lots of people chatting away, eating having a good time, enjoying their food & high school students working.*]

CUT TO:
DINING AREA:

[*Eli is managing things, directing people, others keep patting him on the back, saying way to go... nice job, etc., keep up the good work... thanks for stopping the riot, etc. Eli turns to John the Elder, an older retiree type but is met by a party of three.*]

TYDE
Eli... great job at the town meeting... I love you guys!

MARILYN
You definitely should run for town council.

ELI
Thanks, but I've got my hands full running this place.

MARY
Well, think about it. We could sure use ya.

[*Eli walks over to a table, Marie and her two young teens are having lunch, gives her a kiss on the cheek and a light hug.*]

ELI
Hey guys... how ya doing?

[*girl is wearing a soccer uniform and texting her boyfriend, younger boy is playing a game on cell phone and Marie's phone is beeping a couple of times during conversation, she shows phone to Eli...*]

MARIE
It's him, Kevin... it's getting worse.

ELI
You gotta block his number.

MARIE
Somehow it keeps getting through.

ELI
You may have to go to the police.

[*motioning not to involve the kids.*]

MARIE
ssshhh... we'll talk later.

ELI
I'll meet you at the soccer match... I need to take care of a couple of things around here, first.

MARIE
OkeeDokee.

[*John the Elder walks by and they
walk away from the table.*]

ELI
John, could I see you for a moment?

JOHN THE ELDER
Mr. Eaton, we have a situation in front that needs your touch... could you come help out?

ELI
How many times do I have to tell you, it's Eli.

JOHN THE ELDER
As long as you're my boss, it's Mr. Eaton, thank you very much.

[*walking to the front entrance, some
loud contentious voices are heard.*]

JOHN THE ELDER
Listen... it looks like a party of four just came in insisting they have reservations and another party of three is next in line and the four wants to skip ahead of the three... and both are giving Betty the business.

ELI
Hi, I'm Eli Eaton, the owner, what can I do to help out?

PARTY OF THREE
We've been waiting in line and it's our turn for the next table and this... other group just barged in here demanding to be seated next... that's just not fair.

PARTY OF FOUR
Look, we made reservations for 12:30 and it's 12:30, right on the nose... don't blame us if you didn't make reservations.

[*pointing to sign...*]

ELI
We only take reservations on weekend evenings, with a credit card...

PARTY OF FOUR
We just called an hour ago and no one said anything about that.

BETTY
Mr. E, I'm sorry... someone called before and asked if they could come in at 12:30 and I said sure, no problem.

ELI
OK, sounds like both of you have a point... so here's what I propose. Whichever group is willing to wait for the next table will get free fountain drinks.

PARTY OF FOUR
We'll take you up on that offer.

ELI
Fantastic, everyone... enjoy your meals.

BETTY
Thanks Mr. E.

[*walking away with John...*]

ELI

Amazing how quickly people change their attitude when they get something for free.

JOHN THE ELDER

You do have a way with people.

ELI

Just common sense, Q=R≥E... communicate and mobilize. Anyway, I need to take tomorrow off. I've got Moose covering for me in the kitchen, but I was wondering if you could help out and manage things out here with the guests, while I'm gone?

JOHN THE ELDER

Well, Mr. Eaton, I'd love to... could certainly use the extra money... but, don't think I can.

ELI

What's the problem?

JOHN THE ELDER

It's not that I can't... it's just that I **CAN'T**.

ELI

OK, John, you got me...I'm confused... what's up?

JOHN THE ELDER

I can't make too much money.

[*jokingly.*]

ELI

Have you taken a vow of poverty or something?

JOHN THE ELDER
No... it's the damn Social Security.

ELI
It's not running out yet, is it? I was hoping something would be left when I retire!

JOHN THE ELDER
No, I get my money every month, just fine...it's just that if I make too much, they take away some of my money. Go figure the government.

ELI
Excuse me?

JOHN THE ELDER
I had to retire early due to my heart condition, so I started collecting Social Security at age 62. If I make more than $15,000 a year until I'm 66, they take away my benefits.

[*clearly agitated.*]

ELI
Whaaat? That's nuts. You know... that kind of bullshit really makes me crazy.

JOHN THE ELDER
And that's not the half of it. I could have a million dollars worth of bank interest and it wouldn't affect my social security one iota... but if I earn a salary more than a lousy $15,000 a year... lookout... I get socked. The fat cats always get the steak, us little folks only get the scraps.

[*shaking his head in disbelief.*]

ELI

Let me get this straight... so if you retire early and don't pay any more into the system, you're OK, but if you work and keep paying into social security, you get screwed on your benefits until you're 66?

JOHN THE ELDER
Yup. You got it.

ELI

That is just sooo wrong. Someone's gotta do something about this insanity. John, my man... is there any way we can make this work.

[sheepishly.]
JOHN THE ELDER
You could pay me cash... under the table. I know the Pub down the road has some illegals working there in the kitchen and they get paid under the table.

ELI
Geez, I really hate doing stuff like that. And you wonder why we have an immigration problem in this country.

JOHN THE ELDER
I'd love to help out... but I'm caught between a rock and the Social Security office.

[grudgingly.]

ELI

All right... I'm stuck here...guess I don't have any choice. Screw this... OK, see me when your shift is over tonight and I'll take care of you.

JOHN THE ELDER
Thanks a lot, Mr. Eaton... I won't let you down.

ELI
Thanks, John.

CUT TO:

SOCCER FIELD, GIRLS MATCH:

[*Eli is setting up his chair and sits down next to Marie.*]

ELI
What's the score?

MARIE
One nothing. Gabby scored it.

ELI
My luck... all the time we sit here... and she scores a goal the one time I'm not here!

[*showing Eli her cell phone.*]

MARIE
He's been texting the kids.

ELI
Geez, come on...that's gotta stop.

MARIE
I know.

ELI

If we're going to have the family meeting on Sunday and tell the kids we're getting married, you need to tell him in no uncertain terms to let it go already.

MARIE

He wants to meet me... one last time.

ELI

You think that's a good idea?

MARIE

If I'm going to wake up next to you every day, for the rest of my life, I need to end this thing the right way.

ELI

Well, I like the idea of waking up next to each other every morning... but...

[*grabbing his arm and pulling him
closer.*]

MARIE

Yeah, that does sound nice.

ELI

Do whatever you need to... but I don't like it.

MARIE

I'll take care of it, trust me.

ELI

You're not the one I'm worried about. By the way... should we include Matt in the meeting, or should I just tell him tonight?

MARIE

Probably better to tell him. Might be a good idea to have him at the meeting, too... the kids are all going to have to get along when he's home from college.

[*everybody is cheering... another goal
is scored and Eli's cell phone rings.*]

ELI

Sorry, it's the restaurant ... I better take this.
[*Eli nodding.*] Yeah, John...Uh huh... Uh huh... Uh huh... can I talk to this guy?... OK... ahhh... I'll leave now... be there in a couple minutes. [*ends call.*] Got an emergency back at the restaurant... some guy is trying to close the restaurant down because of some zoning violation nonsense.

[*Eli leaves while Marie tapping on her
cell phone.*]

CUT TO:

6. Getting Screwed

PIKNIK*S RESTAURANT:

*[yellow tape over door to PIKNIK*S...*
both councilmen are smirking and the
Police Captain is standing in front of
entrance.]

POLICE CAPTAIN [MILLER]
Mr. Eaton, I have a warrant here which calls for closing down all business activity on this property until all zoning violations are resolved... I'm sorry.

ELI
What's the problem? I've been in business here for over 15 years... nothing has changed.

MILLER
A young man was reported injured earlier when a vehicle exiting this property ran into him. We're required to investigate and apparently, there is an issue with an inadequate number of parking spaces for the size of this property. I've just measured things out and the violations check out. Again, I'm sorry, but I have no option but to enforce this warrant. Get an attorney and see what you can do, although I don't see how you can do it, without tearing down half the restaurant and re-designing the whole back section over that way.

[disgusted and knowing the first
councilman is behind all this.]

ELI

Yeah... an attorney... right. Do you have any idea how much money I'm losing every hour this place is out of commission? Fresh food, people's wages?

MILLER

Again... I am sorry. I have no choice.

[first councilman smugly gives thumbs up to second councilman, as they are about to leave the property Eli fakes a lunge toward the councilmen in fake anger, just to startle them but the Police Captain holds him back with one arm.]

MILLER [CONT'D]

Whoa Eli... that's no way to deal with this... get your lawyer and appeal it.

[local TV station crew wants to interview Eli since the business is popular, also reporter has some unconfirmed information about the accident.]

TV REPORTER

Mr. Eaton... Luis Hernandez, NBC TV 33 News. Could I speak with you for a comment?

ELI

Can we do this a little later?

TV REPORTER

OK, but I've received some unconfirmed information... about an accident here earlier that might have been staged.

7. Can't Get No Relief

FADE IN:

COURTHOUSE HALLWAY:

[*Friday morning.*]

[*Eli and his attorney, Arnie are sitting waiting to go before Judge Curtis.*]

ELI
Geez, I really hate this place.

ARNIE
Bad memories from all the custody hearings?

[*lamenting.*]
ELI

Ten years of non-stop hearings, motions, contempt trials... I never thought I'd have to set foot in this place again.   At least we'll have a different judge. We **ARE** going to have a different judge, aren't we?

ARNIE
Oh yeah, this isn't family court...Judge Curtis is pretty good. Hey, last time you were here wasn't so bad... you got full custody of Matt.

ELI
That was the only time I ever walked out of this building without feeling like I needed a shower.

ARNIE
So what's this I hear about you and Marie back together?

ELI
Yeah, a few months ago she started showing up and things started up again. We just agreed to get married in a few months, if she can sell her house.

ARNIE
Well, I hope things work out better this time.

ELI
Everything should be fine, now... I don't have all the custody crap hanging over my head now, Matt isn't a minor anymore and I can concentrate on Marie and the kids. We just have to deal with an ex-boyfriend.

BAILIFF
Counselor, you'll will be on deck shortly.

ARNIE
Thanks, Tom.

ELI [CONT'D]
... and this guy, Kevin has been coming around hassling her, even contacting the kids... apparently he's the guy she hooked up with after our engagement fell apart a couple years ago.

ARNIE
Everything OK with the two of you?

ELI
Oh, yeah... She just can't seem to get rid of him. She agreed to see him tonight and tell him in no uncertain terms to leave her and the kids alone.

ARNIE
You think that's a good idea?

ELI
No... but she'll call when she gets back home. Hey, it's our poker night, and I'll be so distracted you can win all my money. I'm sure you won't mind.

ARNIE
Anything to help out a friend! Hi Marie.

[Marie arrives, Eli gets up, they briefly hug and kiss on the cheek.]

ELI
Thanks for coming... I can use your support.

[showing a bit of withdrawal, distraction.]

MARIE
Hi Arnie...It's OK... I'll have to get back, Zack is home sick... he's sleeping... but I've got some time. I'd like to help.

BAILIFF
Counselor, you're on deck... one case before you.

ARNIE
OK, Let's go in... remember, let me do all the talking, no colorful language and don't you dare make any facial expressions... and don't roll your eyes... no matter what you hear!

ELI

Yeah... Yeah... You sound just like my mother... stand up straight... make sure your zipper is closed... talk clearly... don't make facial expressions... don't roll your eyes... I'm surprised you didn't tell me to straighten my coat and tie my shoelaces.

[being Eli's poker buddy...]

ARNIE

Straighten your coat, tie your shoelaces... and speaking of straightening... never draw to an inside straight.

[straightens his jacket and points to his shoes.]

MARIE
Here... There.

[Eli proceeds to tie his shoe laces.]

CAMERA FOLLOWS GROUP
INTO THE COURTROOM:

[door to courtroom opens, they enter and sit down on one of the benches as 3 people are walking out glassy eyed.]

BAILIFF
Parties come forward for the Commonwealth versus Jeffers.

*[DA, public defender and a **wheel chair bound** middle aged man dressed in wrinkled unkempt clothing with a guard proceed in front of Judge Curtis.]*

*[looking down with his reading glasses
at his folder, not seeing the parties
coming up to the bench.]*

JUDGE CURTIS
Let's see here... Commonwealth versus Barney Jeffers...
hearing for bail on a charge of armed robbery of a bank... the
Defendant has already pleaded not guilty.

*[Judge Curtis finally looks up and does
a double take that the Defendant is in
a wheel chair and then speaking to the
DA, using his hand to gesture toward
the Defendant.]*

JUDGE CURTIS
Am I to assume that this gentleman here is the Defendant...
Mr. Jeffers?
DA
Yes, your Honor.

JUDGE CURTIS
And am I to further assume that the Defendant was **NOT**
confined to a wheelchair at the time of the... alleged... armed
robbery.

DA
No, your Honor... the... ah... Defendant was indeed in his
wheelchair at the time of the robbery.

JUDGE CURTIS
Really... and here I thought today's docket was going to be
just another boring day at the office.

ELI
And we have to follow this?

*[looking sternly at Eli, Arnie and
Marie give him a sharp elbow to the
midsection.]*

BAILIFF
Quiet in the courtroom!

JUDGE CURTIS
Hmmm...I was just going to read... the report... but now... I think I'd prefer hearing the details from you.

*[holding up a clear plastic evidence
bag.]*

DA
Your Honor, Mr. Jeffers is accused of... well, rolling... into the Forrest Park branch of the Bank of Massachusetts at 4:32 PM, brandishing this weapon and demanding $142.36 from the teller, or that he would quote... 'take care of her'.

JUDGE CURTIS
I'm amazed that the bank was open so late... anyway... do continue, *[waiving his hand.]* please.

DA
The teller proceeded to hand over $142.50, Mr. Jeffers then threw $.14 back at her and spun around and wheeled out of the bank and down Sumner Ave. in a westerly direction. We have the security footage with a beautiful shot of the Defendant in the bank and a video shot from a witness's cell phone as the police were chasing him down Sumner Ave. We're here today to establish a flight risk and bail.

JUDGE CURTIS

I'm sure there must be a great story as to why the amount was 142 dollars... [pause, shaking his head.] and 36 cents... and that he made change, but unfortunately, that will have to wait for the trial, and I can only hope I'll be assigned to the case... but today we are only concerned with...

BACK SHOT OF
PARTIES BEFORE JUDGE:

[*the lights flicker as though a
brownout is imminent.*]

JUDGE CURTIS [CONT'D]

We were warned there might be a brownout today... don't be alarmed... as I was saying... we are only concerned with bail and the possible risk of flight.

[*lights, scene go black, meanwhile in
the dark...*]

BAILIFF

Everybody stay calm, don't move.. we'll have power back shortly... we have a backup generator ready.

ELI

This is better than reality TV!

[*after a short while, noisy shuffling,
mumbling, the lights come on,
continue with back shot, but now the
Defendant in the wheelchair is
conspicuously missing, but the DA
doesn't notice. As the lights come back
on, the DA, a real trooper, continues
with his argument.*]

DA

So your honor, we are asking for $10,000 bail under the circumstances, we feel there may be a flight risk.

[*calmly looking around... surveying
the situation and then speaking to the
DA.*]

JUDGE CURTIS

Strangely, I'm inclined to agree with you on this one. Oh... by the way... are you aware the Defendant... [*spreading his arms out.*] is no longer with us?!?

[*oddly, no one really noticed and every
one freezes looking around and at
each other. Eli jokingly looks under
the bench, Arnie and Marie give him
another elbow to the midsection
when... Mr. Jeffers comes calmly
wheeling back into the entrance of the
courtroom.*]

[*in an uncharacteristically refined
voice, compared to his clothing, he
sees the stunned faces all around him
and everyone frozen in their tracks.*]

JEFFERS

Well, nature called... and I didn't want to inconvenience any one.

[*he quickly wheels back to his original
position before the Judge.*]

JUDGE CURTIS
Thanks for re-joining us Mr. Jeffers.

JEFFERS
My pleasure... your Honor.

[*Judge Curtis nods to the Bailiff, who slowly moves to guard the door and calls on his walkie-talkie for backup support.*]

JUDGE CURTIS
Does defense counsel have anything to add?

[*holding up the evidence bag, he takes out a clear plastic water gun filled with Gatorade and squirts it.*]

PUBLIC DEFENDER
Your Honor... this is the 'armed' part of the alleged robbery.

[*looking at Jeffers.*]

JUDGE CURTIS
A water gun?

JEFFERS
Well, it was a rather hot day. And it was filled with lemon-lime Gatorade... electrolytes and all... one needs to be properly hydrated during exercise, especially when confined to a wheel chair.

JUDGE CURTIS
Like escaping from the police?

[*Jeffers gives a grudging shrug.*]

JUDGE CURTIS [CON'TD]
OK... I just can't help myself... what's the deal with the 142 dollars... and 36 cents?

[Public Defender looking at Jeffers.]

PUBLIC DEFENDER
If one... were to admit to this event... and we are not doing so at this time, your honor.

JUDGE CURTIS
Of course.

JEFFERS
There was an unfortunate delay in processing my Social Security check and the bank failed to properly credit my account in a timely manner, so when my check to the electric company in the amount of $142.36 bounced... due to insufficient funds... according to the bank... through no fault of my own, I might add... the electric company unceremoniously terminated my power. As I said, it was a very hot day... global warming and all, with an extremely high humidity index... naturally, nerves were frayed.

JUDGE CURTIS
I see. Mr. Jeffers, I admire your sense of justice, fair play... and your desire for air conditioning. However, I cannot condone such behavior. There are, however two points that must be considered. First the amount in question is under $250, the statutory amount for a felony... *[looking at Jeffers.]* thankfully Mr. Jeffers, your electric bill was not higher... and second, given the nature of the implement, as a matter of law, the court cannot find there was any felonious criminal intent to inflict substantive bodily harm with a clear plastic water gun... filled with lemon-lime Gatorade.

JEFFERS
If it makes a difference, your Honor, it was sugar free.

[*the clerk, off to the side of the Judge*
Curtis points to a huge folder.]

JUDGE CURTIS [CONT'D]
Aah yes... I almost forgot... the witness who shot the video of you... excuse me... the accused... barreling down Sumner Ave with the police in hot pursuit... he uploaded the video to You Tube... and it apparently has gone viral... we have received in excess of 10,000 e-mails demanding clemency for Mr. Jeffers.

JUDGE CURTIS [CONT'D]
This may work in reality TV... or politics... but this type of pressure brought to bear will not influence any decision of this court. Mr. Jeffers, given that the maximum offense chargeable by law is a misdemeanor, I hereby order you to be held over for trial... and that bail be set to insure your return to court in the amount of...ooh, say... $142.36. You may make arrangements with the Bailiff... so ordered.

[*Judge Curtis taps his gavel, parties*
exit and the Bailiff stands up
announcing...]

BAILIFF
The cases of Eaton versus the Town of West Longmeadow and Koepeknie versus Eaton.

[*Arnie, Eli and Rippner, attorney for*
Koepeknie walk up to the bench.]

JUDGE CURTIS

I see we have two motions before the court this morning... both relating to the same incident... is that correct?

ARNIE

That is correct your Honor. Sadly, I doubt this matter will rise to the drama of the previous case.

JUDGE CURTIS

Sadly, indeed... but the show must go on. Let's deal first with the Motion to Stay Execution of the Closure of PIKNIK*S restaurant at 138 Main Street. I may have to recuse myself from this case... my family loves to eat there... frequently. Let's see where this goes, before I make any decision on that aspect... as I recollect, the other Justices of this Court also frequent that establishment for lunch.

ARNIE

Your Honor, the Zoning Enforcement Officer from West Longmeadow   enforced the closure of PIKNIK*s restaurant, at the aforementioned address, due to a recently enacted Zoning By-Law which purports to require a minimum number of parking spaces, along with a minimum amount of space for ingress and egress from the commercial property, all under the auspices of public safety. Mr. Eaton, the owner has been operating his PIKNIK*S restaurant at this location without incident for the past fifteen years. The problem now, is that PIKNIK*S uses only fresh food... nothing frozen... and it...

JUDGE CURTIS

Thanks, but the court doesn't need to hear an advertisement... I am aware of that.

ARNIE

Sorry Judge, but If the restaurant does not re-open immediately, all the food inventory will be lost, causing irreparable loss and damage to Mr. Eaton, along with the loss of jobs both full time and part time of nearly 40 people, trying to make a living. We are asking the Court to stay the order to close, pending a final determination of the alleged zoning infraction and whether PIKNIK*S should be grandfathered under the new Zoning By-Law.

JUDGE CURTIS

I have in the folder a certified copy of the zoning ordinance and a certified copy of the West Longmeadow Police Department that measurements were taken indicating a clear violation, and taking into account the other case before us this morning, apparently there is now an issue of public safety.

ARNIE

We acknowledge that there has been an alleged incident leaving the property, but our concern is the validity of the recently enacted By-Law as it applies to grandfathering an operating facility actively in business for 15 years prior to this new By-Law.

JUDGE CURTIS

Unfortunately counselor, the By-Law makes no mention of grandfathering any previously operating businesses. Given the circumstances of a physical injury having occurred on the property, I don't have any flexibility. Let me hear argument on the second related case... this involves a MOTION TO DISMISS action that the injured party is suing PIKNIK*S and Mr. Eaton as owner for contributory negligence... for violation of the Zoning By-Law. Is that correct?

ATTORNEY RIPPNER

That is correct your Honor, we believe there is a prima facie case of negligence here based upon the violation of the By-Law in question.

JUDGE CURTIS

I see that the injury took place on October 12, 2015?

ARNIE

That is correct.

JUDGE CURTIS

I also see that the Zoning By-Law was passed on October 11, 2015?

ATTORNEY RIPPNER

That is correct.

JUDGE CURTIS

Hmmm. Curious. I also see that the Attorney General has not ratified the By-Law as of today?

ATTORNEY RIPPNER

Aaah, that appears to also be correct.

JUDGE CURTIS

Looks like my decision is clear in both cases... as painful as it is... I love their cheeseburgers... I must rule that the MOTION TO STAY must be denied and the order to close PIKNIK*S be upheld... and the MOTION TO DISMISS must be allowed, also, since the By-Law was not ratified until **AFTER** the incident, as a matter of law there can be no inference of negligence by Mr. Eaton or PIKNIK*S as of the date of the accident... so ordered. *[He taps the gavel.]* Aahh... I love it when we finish by lunchtime... and I have a sudden urge for a cheeseburger and nowhere to go, now! I may end up regretting my last decision.

BAILIFF

Please step away from the bench... There will be a lunch recess of one hour... All rise.

ELI

That's it?

ARNIE

We got one out of two... could've been worse.

ELI

That may work in baseball, but what the hell do I do with the restaurant... This will bankrupt me unless I close it up. I can't afford to tear down the restaurant and re-build. Insurance won't cover this. I'm going to have to let everyone go... all because of those bastards at town hall? What a nightmare. Tell me we can appeal this decision?

ARNIE

Sure, but it could take weeks, months or even years to resolve on appeal. Just think how long the N.F.L. Deflategate has been dragging on in appeal and it's still not resolved, because the appeal can be appealed... and let's face it, you're not Tom Brady. You know I'm not one to give in, but this is a situation that has you caught between a rock and city hall... and in this case, you can't fight city hall.

[*after a rather long pause, trying to*
digest the reality...]

ELI

So I'm screwed, no matter what... and that's it? [*pause.*] You know, I could actually deal with this, on my own, but all my employees? They're like family... this sucks!

ARNIE

Eli, if you can handle the food inventory, I'll handle everything else for you, the equipment, the employees, the building and liquidate everything. Does your CPA have access to your business computer so I can coordinate things for you?

ELI

Yeah, just call Bill. He'll give you access to any information you need to tie up any loose ends. I'll notify all the employees and you'll have to deal with all the unemployment comp claims that I'm sure will be filed. Let me know if you need anything else. *[dejected.]* Thanks, Arnie... you're the best.

ARNIE

OK... You'll be at the poker game tonight, right?

ELI

Geez, I should just give you my credit card and forget it. *[sighing...]* Yeah, I'll be there.

CUT TO:

8. LEMONS

PIKNIK*S RESTAURANT:

[*Eli is sitting at a table in the empty restaurant for a few moments. He then picks up a phone and makes a call to the local food bank.*]

ELI

... yeah, I've got all this food here and I don't want it to go to waste. Sure, if you could send a truck over right away... yeah... most of it is refrigerated. I'm happy to help out... thanks, but it looks like we're going to have to close up for good. Ok, I'll see you in an hour.

[*a group of somber employees come into the restaurant and walk up to Eli. They all hug each other without saying anything.*]

JOHN THE ELDER

Is it true... what we've heard... we're closing up... for good?

ELI

I'm afraid so... the Judge wouldn't let us stay open.

BETTY

Is there any other place around here we can go to?

ELI

There's nothing close to this size anywhere within 25 miles, just a couple small strip mall places.

JOHN THE ELDER
Mr. E, what are we going to do?

ELI
My lawyer will be in touch with everyone... he'll help everyone with any unemployment comp claims you have to file.

JOHN THE ELDER
I don't mind telling you... this is not right.

ELI
Nothing I can do. I am so sorry. Here are your final paychecks. Bring it in... I just want to thank everyone for everything you've done over the years... Hey, I couldn't have done it without ya's. I'm really going to miss you all. You're family.

[*everyone huddles together.*]

FADE OUT:

9. Life is a Gamble

FADE IN:
DEN, ROUND TABLE WITH GUYS
PLAYING TEXAS HOLD'EM POKER:

[*cards are being dealt, chips are being
tossed in, hands are being laid down,
chips are being collected during the
conversation.*]

ELI
Hey, Arnie, just wanted to thank you for everything this
morning.

ARNIE
Happy to help out... just sorry we couldn't keep PIKNIK*S
open.

J.K.
Whaaat? I didn't hear... what happened to PIKNIK*S?

ELI
A couple of a-holes from town hall had the restaurant closed
up for violating some bullshit new zoning law. I think they
staged an accident in retaliation for my standing up against
them at the last town meeting.

YAZ
Wow... I'm sorry to hear that? But that won't stop me from
raising you a dollar.

ELI
No respect... no respect I tell you... I call.

J.K.
What are you going to do?

ELI
I could appeal the Judge's decision, but that could take months... years, without any guarantee of success... and I'd go bankrupt in less than a week, unless I close it up immediately.

A.Z.
That sucks... big time. Where in the hell am I gonna get a good cheeseburger and fries now?

J.K
Yeah...no shit.

YAZ
Arnie, I've never seen you give up before.

ARNIE
Even if they made up the whole freakin' accident, they've got the power... you just can't fight city hall. Time is the enemy here. They've got you over a barrel by dragging it out. One guy like Eli, against the system doesn't have a chance in the short term.

[*close up on Eli, who pauses after that comment, looks up into space and gives a slight smile, as though he is remembering something.*]

GREG
So Eli, what are you gonna do?

ELI

Looks likes I'll be gettin married... with three kids... maybe this is a blessing... I couldn't do both and maintain my sanity.

GREG

Whoa... married? When did this happen?

ELI

Marie and I have gotten back together over the past few months and we're going to give it a second try. You know what they say... second time's a charm.

BOB

I think that's the third time.

ELI

Whatever, I call... you're bluffing.

[*Eli tentatively looks at his cell phone for a text message from Marie... but nothing.*]

FADE OUT:

10. Making Lemonade

FADE IN:
INSIDE OF ELI'S HOME:

[*midnight, after poker game, Eli plops downs into his recliner chair and gazes out into space, realizing he has nothing to do in the morning without the restaurant, then hearing nothing from Marie, decides to drive by her house and sees his car parked in the driveway, lights out. He then texts Marie and just shakes his head, dejected and drives home...*]

ELI'S CELL PHONE
"???"

ELI
I've got to be an idiot for not seeing this.

[it's now 1am, Eli goes to his closet, opens a box with file folders, fingers through half of the box and pulls out a folder and takes a college term paper out of the folder, glances at it and tosses it on an end table next to his recliner... the title reads...Poli Sci 101 "How Can I Make a Difference?" Subtititled: "I'm Going to Run for Vice President, That's How!" By Eli Eaton. Eli brings a snack from the kitchen, plops down and begins to read the paper. Now we can see handwriting in red ink on the second page. "A" "Best paper I've read in years... a provocative concept, a genuine paradigm shift...elegant plan. You should really do this some day!" Eli falls asleep in the recliner with his cell phone on his lap.]

[*Eli wakes up the next morning in the recliner, immediately checks his cell phone to find no message or call from Marie and goes to the computer to check email... nothing. He shakes his head and throws his cell phone into the recliner, rather dejected.*]

[*muttering to himself.*]

ELI
An idiot I am, Sam.

ELI'S KITCHEN:

[*cell phone showing three hours passed and then it beeps... a text from Marie.*]

ELI'S CELL PHONE
Kevin is over here with the kids   call u later   can't do lunch I'm sorry.

[*Eli texts back.*]

We're supposed to announce engagement tomorrow w kids and ur w Kevin w kids??? I just lost restaurant and ur telling me all this via text? How millennial of you! grow up! BTW... doubt ur sorry. Obviously u were just using me these past months.

[*Eli receives another text.*]

That's mean!
[*Eli texts back.*]

Really ur accusing me of being mean... that's rich. Don't bother calling... I'm done. Burn me once, shame on thee... twice... shame on me.

[*he tosses the phone back into the recliner. The phone beeps again, but he ignores it, then picks it up later and texts his son...*]

ELI'S CELL PHONE
Hey, can u stop by tomorrow... got news.

Roget dat. 11 OK?

OK

FADE OUT AND BACK IN:

[*Sunday morning at 11AM, Matt, Eli's son walks in the door with a huge load of laundry. Eli goes to give him a big hug, but the laundry gets in the way.*]

ELI
Matt... am I glad to see you.

MATT
It hasn't been that long. I came as soon as I could.

ELI
I know... thanks.

MATT
So what's going on with the restaurant?

ELI
Who said anything about the restaurant?

MATT
Dad... when you're like this, it's **ALWAYS** about the restaurant.

ELI
So you think you're so smart, eh? Well it's only half about the restaurant. The police just shut down the restaurant because of some zoning law bullshit... the town councilmen a-holes are trying to get back at me for talking up against something they wanted at the town meeting last week.

[*Matt is visibly shocked.*]

MATT
Whoa... didn't see that coming. Oh wait, you're pranking me, right?

ELI
Oh, and then Marie just dumped me for this other guy.

MATT
Man, now I know you're pranking me!

[*Eli just stares at him, then Matt slowly realizes this is not prank.*]

OMG... you're not kidding, are you? What happened, she get cold feet?

ELI
More like fast feet...looks like she's running off with an old boyfriend, or better yet, looks like he's already moved in over there.

MATT

Holy crap! That's unbelievable. I thought you were getting engaged... again. Geez, at least you won't have to help raise another two kids... they are a handful.

ELI

Actually, as pissed off as I am, I feel worse for Zack and Gabby.

MATT

I didn't want to say anything, but I just saw her with some guy at Dunkin Donuts this morning getting coffee.

ELI

Really? If this were a movie, you'd say, totally not believable.

MATT

What are you going to do?

ELI

Eat... You hungry?

MATT

Really?... I'm a college student.

ELI

Let's crack some eggs.

CUT TO:
KITCHEN:

[*Face the Press is on a TV playing in background as they make food and eat* .]

TV ANNOUNCER
...Face the Press... with Mike Rudd

ELI
Son, don't ever give up your dream for someone else.

MATT
You're just pissed off now.

ELI
I am, but I'm serious...   *[To the TV while people are talking...]* That is a total non-sequitur! What is the matter with those people?!

MATT
Dad, you've always told me to go for my dreams...to get along with people and never intentionally hurt anyone along the way.

ELI
I still feel that way, just don't rely on anyone else for your happiness. Remember the Q formula. *[to the TV.]* ...and you call that syllogistic reasoning?

MATT
Oh God, not the Q formula again, please!

ELI
Sometimes you have a dream when you're young, and then life throws you a curve ball and before you know it, everything you've been hoping for goes up in smoke like that

[snapping his fingers, then to the TV.]

I swear, these guys in office never saw someone else's dollar that they didn't want to spend. I'd like to see them do it with their own money... Listen to me son, whenever you have a dream, do whatever you can to go for it. It may or may not work out, but you've at least gotta give it a try... and yes, you gotta use the Q formula.

MATT
So... what has been your dream?

ELI
Sounds crazy, but I've always wanted to run for office, ever since college. When you watch those idiots on TV act like spoiled brats, it just drives me nuts... the bickering with each other, they always have to get their way, just to get TV time... Someone with common sense has to step up and jump in there and shake things up... someone who doesn't want to line his own pockets. Did you see 60 Minutes last week, all the Congressmen selling stock on insider information?... it just sucks.

MATT
It's the system, Dad.

ELI
Someone has to change it.

MATT
Sounds idealistic... do you really think you could run for Congress? Nothing personal, but you would need political connections, backers, a party... and you are an independent... but what you really need... is gobs of   M O N E Y.

ELI

See, that's what I'm talking about. If you have a dream, you should be able to figure a way to do it, without getting beat down by the system. Listen, if I were to travel for a few months, now that I don't have to worry about PIKNIK*S anymore, or Marie for that matter... would you be OK with that?

MATT

Sure, I'll be in the dorm until next May, and Mom is still around.

ELI

Yeah, I know... I just don't want you to think I was abandoning you.

MATT

Dad, after all you went through with custody, I doubt that... I mean, like, where would you be going... to Antarctica?

ELI

Hmmm, penguins... that would be cool... I gotta get there one day, but no, I mean jumping in the car and just take off, driving cross country and back, kinda like that TV commercial.

MATT

Sounds like a great time... How 'bout I join you during break?

ELI

Yeah, that would be cool... I would like that.

MATT

And what would you be doing, exactly?

ELI
Well, I guess you're right... I can't realistically run for
Congress... but then, why should I settle for that?

MATT
Settle? Huh? ...Then, what will you be doing?

[*a noticeable look comes over his face
as though he has had an epiphany.*]

ELI
You know... **I'm** going to be that someone. I'm going to be
the neutron!

MATT
Doing what...?

ELI
Something I've wanted to do since being a freshman in
college...

[*holding up and pointing to his college
paper.*]

ELI
Running for Vice President of the United States!

HOLD SHOT FOR A MOMENT:

SLOW FADE OUT THEN FADE IN:
CUT TO:

ELI'S DEN:

[Eli is reviewing his notes, plotting out a map, making notes, planning a trip from Maine to California and back.]

CUT TO:

11. You Can Get There From Here

EXTERIOR OF ELI'S HOUSE:

[Eli is pulling away from the house in his SUV, driving on the Interstate through Boston, to Maine to start his cross country journey from Maine to California and back. [Simon and Garfunkel All come to Look for America playing in background. Show road signs in Concord, Lexington, Boston, Entering Maine.]

CUT TO:

INTERIOR OF MAINE DINER:

[Maine Diner in Kennebunkport, ME, the home of Bush 41. Eli thinks this is a good place to start and is talking with two people sitting in a booth eating lobster... with bibs on.. cracking the claws.]

ELI

Hi... I'm Eli Eaton from Pennsylvania and Massachusetts... and I'm running for Vice President.

[in a thick Maine accent.]

PATRON

Shouldn't ya be campaigning in New Hampsha? Maine doesn't have much relevance in the primaries... or the Electoral College, for that matta.

ELI

I don't need no stinkin primaries...sorry, couldn't resist... but I'd like to think there's a better way.

PATRON
Yaaah, and what would that be?

ELI

Rather than talk and blow a lot of hot air, I'm here to listen...
to find out what's important to you... and eventually take that
to Washington and make a real difference in the everyday
lives of Americans.

PATRON

Sounds, good, but I doubt that could eva happen. You
should know that nuthin' ever gets done in Washington.

ELI

Maybe not... but just maybe... but guess what, this is my
very first stop on a long journey across this country and I'd
love to hear what's on your mind.

[*middle aged husband and wife look at
each other, shrug their shoulders
and...*]

PATRON

Well, since you asked... I'm going to be retire'n in a few years
and I'd like to be sure that Social Security is still gonna be
there... I'm gonna need it to get by. Besides, I've been puttin
into Social Security for ova thirty years now, and I'd like to
see some of my money back. Don't mind paying taxes, as
long as I see the money going somewhere other than some
big black hole in Washington.

ELI

You don't mind if I write this down... do ya?

PATRON

Be my guest.

ELI

And let me ask you a question... if you pay the same amount of taxes, would you rather it be deducted from your paycheck... or paid when you buy stuff... no more, no less after all is said and done?

[*thinking for a couple moments, rubbing his chin...*]

PATRON

Guess I'd rather pay it when I buy something, that way at least I have some choice in the matta.

ELI

And having a choice is important to you... kind of like choosing from a menu?

PATRON
Yaah. Sure.

[*server walks by, Eli writing in a notebook, talking to the server.*]

ELI
Would you mind taking our picture together?

SERVER
Sure thing, hon. You need to get a selfie stick!

[*server takes picture with Eli's cell phone and hands it back to Eli.*]

ELI

Thanks. I'm Eli Eaton from Pennsylvania and Massachusetts and I'm running for Vice President.

SERVER
Well good luck to ya. You married?

ELI
Well, thanks... and no.

[*taking a picture from her pocket and showing to Eli...*]

SERVER
This is my younger sister, she's really a looker, wouldn't ya say?

[*a bit flustered and a bit surprised.*]

ELI
Well, yeah... she really is attractive.

SERVER
Here's her numbah... you should give her a call.

ELI
Thanks... I think... is there anyone else you know in the restaurant who likes talking about politics?

SERVER
Oh boy, do I. Just come with me and I'll introduce ya to a baby you can kiss. That's what you politicians do isn't it?

CAMERA PANS ACROSS DINER:

ELI
Guess so, I'm kinda new at this. Kissing babies, not holding them. Then I'd like to sit down and try one of those lobster casseroles.

*[server takes Eli over a few tables, she
picks up an infant out of a booster seat
and hands him to Eli, just to see how
he deals with a baby... her sister
probably has kids!]*

*[the server starts the video on her cell
phone, Eli easily takes hold of the
baby, showing he's done it before and
gently kisses the baby on the cheek and
jokingly...]*

SERVER
And let me take a video. I'd like to post it on our Facebook page.

ELI
So young man, will you vote for me if I get to be the Vice President nominee?

*[at the exact moment Eli kisses the
infant, the baby vomits all over his
shirt.]*

ELI
Ooooh geez! You're recording this?

SERVER
You betcha... I'll put it on Facebook before ya know it... You Tube, too! It'll probably go viral! But let's get you cleaned up first.

ELI
On second thought, think I'll pass on that lobster casserole... and just go for a whole lobster.

SERVER
Sounds good to me... I'll call my sister.

SHOT OF COMPUTER SCREEN:
FACEBOOK PAGE WITH ELI AND BABY MESS AND
HEADLINE...

**VP CANDIDATE VISITS MAINE DINER AND GETS A
MOUTHFUL!**

CUT TO:

ELI DRIVING ON INTERSTATE:

[*video montage of Eli stopping for gas, talking in
restaurants, each stop has more people talking than the last,
shots of notable places between ME, MA, CT, NY, NJ, DE,
MD, and PA., road signs, etc.*]

12. Coming Home

PRIMANTI'S RESTAURANT, PITTSBURGH, PA.

[*Eli is sitting, talking to a group of about 10-12 people in a corner of the busy restaurant. Eli stands up, other people pull the chairs out to join in, a crowd gathers...*]

MANAGER
Hey everyone... This is Eli Eaton... he wants to go to Wooshington and he's come dahn tahn here to talk politics... and he's OK, he's a lifelong Steeler fan!

CROWD
Woo Hoo!

ELI
Thanks, everyone. It's nice to be home again in the Steel City!

CROWD
Cheering, whistling, whoops.

ELI

Hi... I'm Eli Eaton... I'm a local boy... and I'm running for Vice President.

CROWD

Boooooo!@#%

ELI

That bad, huh?

CROWD

Laughter.

ELI

OK, then, let's change things... and let the revolution start right here in Pittsburgh, where George Washington had his first military success.

LARRY

Is that why there are only two statues at the airport, George Washington...and Franco Harris?

ELI

Yeah, I noticed that... not sure what it all means. The Revolutionary Inception and the Immaculate Reception... Must involve Devine Intervention.

LARRY

So if you become Vice President, what are you going to do fer us here in the 'Burgh?

ELI

[*pause.*]   Nothin.

CROWD

[*stunned silence.*]   Murmuring.

ELI

That's right. I'm not going to suck up to the voters here in Pittsburgh, in Peoria, in Portland or anywhere for that matter. I'm here to listen... If you want someone in Washington who will play the same old dirty politics, take lobbyist money, then play political favoritism, well count me out... go vote for someone else. But if you'd like to be part of some real change... that puts the welfare of our country first, without the lobbying, the influence peddling and the self promotion, I'd love to have your support.

MAYA

OK... let's see how this really works.

ELI

Go for it.

MAYA

First, just exactly where did you grow up?

ELI

Spent my first 10 years living in Swissvale, right off Church Street, next to the Monongahela, then we moved and I went to high school in Mt Lebanon... lived off Bower Hill Road.

[*holding up a newspaper ad for the supermarket, GIANT EAGLE...*]

MAYA

So how do you pronounce this?

ELI

What... Giant Iggle?!

MAYA

Alright!... Sounds like you speak Pittsburghese!

[*applause, approval, a few people start taking videos with their cell phones, an event is unfolding. A local TV reporter shows up and starts taking video from the back.*]

WILLIE

OK, so are you pro union or pro management?

ELI

Geez, thanks for starting off with the easy stuff!

[*laughter from crowd.*]

ELI [CONT'D]

To answer your question honestly, I'm pro nobody.

[*crowd not happy, some boos.*]

WILLIE

There ya go, typical politician.

ELI

Not really... If I was a typical politician I'd lie my ass off and say I was pro union, Pittsburgh having a long history of unions and all, am I right?

WILLIE

Well, yeah, I guess.

[*after a pause, crowd again responding favorably.*]

ELI [CONT'D]

Here's the deal... Remember, I'm running for Vice President, not President. So who can tell me what the Vice President does?

CHERYL

Besides going to funerals? Not much.

ELI [CONT'D]

Exactly! That's my point. I'm running because I think the Vice President is the most underutilized job in the entire government and I want to change that. I believe the Vice President should be independent from the President and should have specific responsibilities and answer to the people and not just be the President's yes man.

[*applause.*]

CHERYL

OK, so what exactly would you do.

ELI

Well, first, I'd go out and buy a black suit, just in case... you know, for funerals.

[laughter from crowd.]

I see the Vice President being independent and bi-partisan, working for "We the People" not a political party like the Democrats or the Republicans. There's already too much drinking the spiked punch in Washington, anyway.

First, I would pressure Congress to vote and agree on the top 10 most important issues facing our country, kinda like David Letterman, *[some chuckling.]* which need immediate attention like tax reform or immigration reform and then, as an independent bi-partisan Vice President, I would be responsible for mediating proposed laws between Congress and the White House to make sure compromises are made, legislation is passed and signed into law by the President. It wouldn't be my job to take sides. It wouldn't be my job to propose any new laws or regulations.

It **WOULD** be my job to manage the domestic legislative process so that things get done and eliminate the gridlock in Washington... and frankly, I think it's better for an outsider to come in and shake things up. That explains Trump's and Carson's poll numbers early on. Anyway, that's why I won't take sides on your union vs. management question. I'm not here to take sides or to make or support any party's politics... I'm here to get things done, whatever the White House and Congress agree needs to get done. *[pause.]* I know getting something done in Washington is a novel concept here, but after 226 years of the Vice President not being much more than a punch line... it's time to communicate and mobilize... $Q=R \geq E$.

BERNIE

Hey Eli, if you get elected, maybe we'll put up another statue at the airport, you along with George and Franco.

[*handing a couple dollars to the server
and acknowledging the guest.*]

ELI

Give my new tall friend here another Iron City... on me! And since I'm not in any primaries, no one can accuse me of buying votes!

ED

So, where's your entourage?

ELI

No entourage, just one guy with a message. Think of me like Johnny Appleseed planting seeds, all around the country... but these seeds are ideas!

TV REPORTER

Mr. Eaton, TV 22... Would you be willing to come down to the station and tape a segment for our Sunday morning news show?

ELI

Love to. But first, let me grab a Primanti's sandwich! Hey... I'm Eaton for Vice President!

13. Motoring

[*video montage showing Eli being interviewed on local TV station [no dialog], driving on the interstate going through WV, OH and MI and stopping in Detroit and arriving at Coney Island Hot Dogs in Detroit. Eli now has a sign which says "I'm Eli Eaton... running for Vice President. What's on your mind? Let's have a chat." Large crowd of people at lunchtime.*]

GUEST [VIRGIE]
Mr. Eaton?

ELI
Please, call me Eli.

GUEST [VIRGIE]

Eli... I work at the Michigan Ford plant... and I'm a member of the UAW. I'm lucky to have a good job, but I seem to be working so hard and when I get my paycheck on Friday, I can't believe how much in taxes they take out... it seems like I'm working for the government... not myself or my family... and now Ford announced that they are no longer going to build Ford Focuses and C-Maxes here anymore in 2018. We may all lose our jobs.

[crowd voices it's approval for the question, people are video recording on their cell phones and there are a couple of more professional type cameras rolling and a couple of reporters taking notes on a laptop.]

ELI

Boy, I can't tell you how many times I've heard that in the past few weeks. The taxes that is, not the plant changes. What's your name?

GUEST
Virgie.

ELI

Virgie, I've been doing a lot of thinking on this issue, as I've been driving from city to city, town to town and this is what I've come up with. This may take a minute or so... are you with me?

VIRGIE
Sure.

ELI

OK. Making a long story short, I'm convinced there needs to be major tax reform in this country. Here's a picture of the IRS tax laws, stacked up next to me.

The stack is almost as tall as I am... and I'm 6'3". Call me crazy, but I think that is just sooo wrong. Now Virgie, I'm not going to stand here and promise all of you that I'm going to get rid of taxes. I'm also not going to tell you we should raise taxes. What I am telling you, is that we need to change **how** we tax people... to make it stupid simple, just to raise the money necessary to keep things going in this country and keep the politics out of it. Now it's real easy to criticize and to blame someone else for a bad situation, but I'd like to propose a common sense solution. Would you like for me to do that, now... cause, this is how I expect to work if elected?

VIRGIE

I've still got a few bites left of my chili dog, go for it.

ELI

Good... by the way, can't wait to try one of those. Anyway, here's my plan. I think it is easier to collect taxes on what we buy, not on what we get paid. I think it makes more sense to tax people on what we take out of the system for our personal benefit, not what we put into it for society's benefit. The tax law should be just like the auto industry right now... moving from gasoline engines to electric or hydrogen motors, we need a hybrid tax system to get us from here to there. So, I am proposing that we consider eliminating most income taxes on wages and salaries for individuals.

[lots of applause.]

ELI [CON'TD]

Not so fast. I know that sounds great, but it's not that easy. If we eliminate income taxes on wages, that money will need to be replaced, and it makes sense adding a national sales tax on things we buy to make up the difference and eliminate all deductions.

CROWD

But that's gonna make everything more expensive to buy!

ELI [CON'TD]

Yes, that's right, but remember, you're going to have more money in your paycheck every week. You will probably end up with the same amount of money in your pocket after all is said and done. The other cool thing about this is that probably 95% of everyone here wouldn't have to file any more tax returns every April 15th. That means we can get the IRS off your back and out of your lives, forever.

[wild cheering.]

REPORTER

Mr. Eaton... I've seen on social media that you're running to only **MANAGE** the domestic legislative process, as an independent bi-partisan Vice President, and not to be suggesting any policy, so why are you talking here about tax policy?

ELI

Good question... I'm only discussing tax reform to show the need for change and to throw out some unconventional ideas to get us off square one for discussion and comparison. Besides, Virgie deserves a straight answer to her question.

REPORTER

OK, that sounds good and all, Mr. Eaton, but aren't sales taxes unfair and regressive?

ELI

It depends. Maybe, but not necessarily. In fact, they could be structured to eliminate any unfairness in the tax system. You just have to exempt food, medicine and basic clothing and scale the rest.

REPORTER

How's that? Sounds too easy to be true.

ELI

How many here believe we should establish a goal to reduce our dependence on foreign oil?

CROWD

Yes!

ELI

OK, now how many people here believe we should reduce our balance of trade deficit?

CROWD
Yes!

ELI
OK, good. Now how many people here believe we should structure our economy to prioritize good paying jobs as one of our top goals.

CROWD
Yes!

ELI
That last one doesn't surprise me here in the Motor City!

CROWD
Cheering.

ELI
OK, so using cars as an example, let's say a consumer has a choice to buy two cars... one is a Bugatti Veyron...

CROWD
Boos.

ELI
Hold on, now... hear me out. The Bugatti gets 8-10 MPG... the lowest MPG of any production vehicle built. And manufacturing a Bugatti doesn't really create any jobs here in the U.S., so in a bi-partisan plan, the Bugatti would have the highest possible sales tax tacked onto its sticker price.

CROWD
Cheering.

ELI

Virgie, you're gonna love my next example. Now let's look at a Ford Focus Electric on the other end of the spectrum.

VIRGIE

Now you're talking. We build those!

ELI

I thought so.. since the Ford Focus electric creates a lot of jobs over at the Michigan plant, at least for the time being, gets the most MPG equivalent of just about any production vehicle available, and best meets our national objectives about foreign oil and trade deficits and jobs, the Ford Focus Electric could have **NO** sales tax added on... and what do you think that would do to Focus sales? Through the roof!

CROWD

[*approvingly.*]   Applause.

ELI

And that should definitely increase jobs to make those cars. So... what we do is implement a sliding scale for the sales tax on stuff we buy. See, it takes politics and un-fairness out of the equation and all taxes would be based on how well the product meets our national objectives. I believe in freedom of choice. You can boo me, but I believe any American citizen has the right to buy a Bugatti Veyron... but if they do, they also have the obligation to pay the stiffest tax to make up for not meeting our national goals as voted on by each Congress.

Now for the kicker, Virgie... If you want to convince Ford not to shift production of the Focus to Mexico, slap a larger sales tax on the foreign built Focus versus a a smaller or no tax on U.S. built Focus and watch how fast they keep production here in Detroit!

CROWD
Lots of applause.

VIRGIE
Thanks, I gotta go now, but I'll vote for you!

ELI
Thank you. Unfortunately you can't vote for me for Vice President, yet, but here's what you **CAN** do...

just ask every presidential candidate who comes by, if they will support the nomination of an independent bipartisan Vice President... hopefully it'll be Eli Eaton!

[after more questions...]

REPORTER
Mr. Eaton, Detroit Gazette could I get you to come down to the office for an interview with the editors?

ELI
Love to... just let me grab a couple of these Coney Island chili dogs, and I'll be right with you. After all, I'm Eaton... for Vice President!

14. Purple is the New Purple

[transition interviewing at Free Press, Detroit News, local TV stations and driving on Interstate to Minneapolis, cutting in shots of Twitter, Facebook, and You Tube... more meetings in restaurants, with more and more people in attendance, finally arriving at the 5-8 Club, home of the Jucy Lucy hamburger. TV station reporters are awaiting his arrival this time, waiting outside anticipating Eli's arrival. Even a couple people with homemade signs "We're Eaton for the VeeP" are being waved around. Faces are painted red and blue and some purple...Eli pulls up and a "We're Eaton for the VeeP" sign in the restaurant's window.]

ELI

Wow... I can't believe this. Are the Jucy Lucy's that good?

CROWD

Yes!!!

ELI

Hi everyone, I'm Eli Eaton, from Pennsylvania and Massachusetts and I'm running for Vice President.

CROWD

[*cheers, mostly from drinking and just
the crowd having a good time.*]

ELI

I'm absolutely blown away to be here in Minneapolis. Let's
go in a have a chat... and a Jucy Lucy burger.

CUT TO:

INTERIOR OF 5-8 CLUB RESTAURANT:

[*large crowd, tables now rearranged
to have Eli sit and talk.*]

ELI

Wow... this is my kind of place... and you all sound like my
kind of people.

[*people are taking pictures, selfies and
videos with cell phones, asking for
autographs, etc.*]

CROWD
Cheers.

GUEST 1
I've been chosen to ask the first question...

ELI
Go for it... please!

GUEST 1

Eli, we're Minnesota purple here, just like our Vikes... hell, we've elected Jesse Ventura and Al Franken... we defy political labels, but one thing we all agree on, we don't spend over budget around here... how can you change Washington's spend and spend more, mentality?

ELI

Let me ask you a question. How many here have borrowed money for a mortgage to buy a house?

CROW

Applause.

ELI

OK... and how many have borrowed money to buy a car?

CROWD

Most, but a slightly fewer applaud.

ELI

As I would expect... so before we get going here, I hope everyone agrees, that for anything big, like homes, cars or businesses, like big money stuff... it's OK to borrow money.

CROWD

OK's

ELI

OK, so my thinking is to have Congress vote specifically what types of things it is OK to borrow money for... schools, roads, bridges, military bases... stuff like that... whatever it may be, Congress should vote for the list, debate it, get advice from their respective states, vote for it and then... and here's the kicker... **stick to it!**

CROWD
Applause.

*[Eli holds up a pie chart showing
allocation of federal budget
expenditures.]*

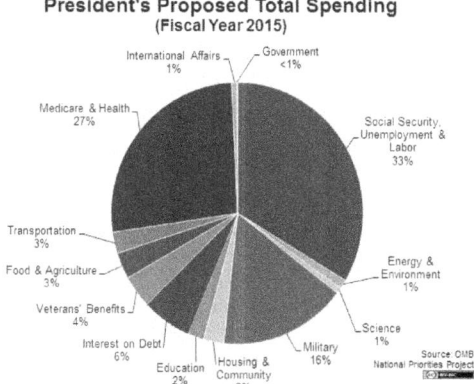

ELI

I hate to sound like a former Presidential candidate with big ears and whose name might rhyme with Thoreau... but I think a pie chart in this case is a good thing.

Look... let's make this stupid simple. The Congress needs to debate and vote on what % of the budget goes to what, period.

Let's just say, for example in the pie chart... Social Security is 33%, Medicare 27% and Military 16% and so on up to 100%. If the government brings in $100 in tax revenue, then Social Security gets $33, Medicare $27 and the Military $16 and so on... you only get a % of what taxes comes in, period. It's the same process for $100 or $1,000,000,000,000. If changes are necessary, it takes a 2/3 vote to make the change due to unforeseen circumstances, but then someone else takes a hit... you can't spend more than 100%, no deficit spending.

All large borrowed expenditures must be prorated out over the life of the asset in the annual budget percentages. We should be living within our means, not gaming the system with lobbyists, special interests and back room deals and tacking spending bills on totally unrelated legislation and then just printing more and more money. Transparency and consistency... top to bottom.

CROWD
Strong approval applause.

[*after more discussion, finally...*]

GUEST 2
OK, I've been volunteered to ask the next question.

ELI
Number two tries harder... go for it.

GUEST 2
We hear you have been running a successful restaurant in Massachusetts for over 20 years now, and please don't take this the wrong way, but what makes you think that running a restaurant, even a successful one, qualifies you to be the Vice President? Are you perhaps being either naive or arrogant?

[*ooohs from the crowd...*]

ELI

Now that is a great question and I hope you think my answer is just as great.

First, you did say you voted for Jesse Ventura, eh? [*a few yeahs.*] and you voted for Al Franken, eh? [*more yeahs.*] so is it a quantum leap from a pro wrestler and a tv comedian to a successful business restaurant owner?... But to honestly address your question... and first, I hope you all agree that I haven't paid anyone here to ask me cream puff questions! [*some laughter.*] I think I'm realistic. Let me ask you this... do you have a family... and what's your name?

GUEST 2 [LOUISE]

Louise, and yeah... a husband and two kids.

ELI

Hi Louise... great, so would you say you are experienced at running your household, protecting your kids, managing a budget, buying a car, arranging for your kid's education...?

LOUISE

Yeah... and it's not easy.

ELI

Oh, I know, but as my professor always told us, the only differences running a large government versus running a family are the number of commas and zeros. He always said, don't be afraid of the commas and zeros, the decisions are the same. The difference in running a $100,000 a year family and a $1 trillion [$1,000,000,000,000] national budget is six extra zeros and three extra commas. You still have to treat people right and resolve differences and conflicts between constituents who honestly see things differently... same thing, period.

LOUISE
Well, that's still a lot of zeros!

ELI
Yes, maybe in sheer volume, but the underlying issues and decisions that need to be made are virtually identical. Let's look at some examples.

[Pointing to the pie chart above.]

The biggest expenditure for the U.S. is 33% for Social Security and unemployment. In my family, we call that an allowance. The only question is what % of our total budget can we afford to spend for living allowances? If 33% is more than we can afford, then we have to make some adjustments, or just have Social Security money be put aside from the general budget... and don't touch it! Medicare is next on the chart with 27%... so Louise, what do you call that in your family?

LOUISE
Aaah, I guess that would be what we spend on health care.

ELI
Exactly, and you have choices, HMO, private doctors or if you really have tons of money, you could pay for concierge doctors who are on call 24/7. The decision is based on what you can afford within your budget? And lastly, 16% is spent for the military... what do you call that in your family?

LOUISE
Our hand guns and burglar alarm?

ELI

Great! As a parent, you need to decide how much is needed for security and protection, given the level of threat to your safety. So as you can see, it all comes back to what we need, what we have to spend and what are our long and short term goals for our 'family'. And let's not forget being a mediator for bickering kids, uncles, grandparents and in-laws... we call them Democrats and Republicans in Washington and foreign countries... so are you getting the picture?

[pauses waiting to see if there is a response.]

The bottom line is... I know you've all heard that size doesn't matter, eh?

[laughter.]

Geez, I can see what's on your minds during the cold Minnesota winters here... but really, it's not about size or the number of zeros, it's all about doing the right thing for the 'family' and if we can get Congress to establish our priorities in writing each and every year, then it becomes nothing more than following a budget, and just doing what's already voted on... whether it's our family or our country... and if things change, then it takes a 2/3 vote.

In the end, it's all about leadership. Our leaders need to have a vision, be able to communicate that vision and then know how to mobilize available resources to make that vision a reality. You don't have to be a professional politician to get the job done. And just to remind everyone, my vision is to make more effective use of the Vice President of the United States by being independent and getting the branches of government to work together, not be at odds with each other all the time. Checks and balances, Yes, gridlock... No!

One last thought... remember, it was the intent of the founding fathers that ordinary citizens come to Washington to serve for a limited time and then return home. This is why George Washington stepped down after two terms as President. If you're unhappy with the current 'professional politicians' in Washington, then I'd appreciate your support.

[*sounds from crowd, OK's, he's right, applause, whistling.*]

REPORTER
Eli... TV 11 News. Could we have a word?

ELI
Love to... just first let me try one of those Jucy Lucys...

CROWD
You'll need a lot of extra napkins!

CUT TO:

15. Life is a Bowl of Sour Dough Chowder

[*transition now showing interviews with all major network affiliates, newspapers, and now You Tube videos popping up all over the place, Instagram photos, Eli doing a Reddit AMA and then Eli hitting the road crossing North & South Dakota, Montana, Washington, Wyoming showing map and shots of more crowds, interviews, etc. in Oregon and ending up in California at San Francisco's Wharf area, again a large crowd, more signs and now some police crowd control... keeps getting bigger and bigger. Eli's visits is now turning into a real draw for all the restaurants and the towns/cities he is showing up at, such that the Mayor is now there.*]

[*show Facebook Screen: "San Francisco... Hey... This is Eli Eaton... I'm running for Vice President... and I'll be visiting the Wharf area next Friday at noon. If you'd like to talk about our country... stop by for a chat."*]

MAYOR YEMANA

Welcome, Eli Eaton... we heard you were coming... so we baked you a... well actually it's an edible sour dough bread bowl... baked fresh right here on the Warf! And I'll bet... everyone here is happy to finally see you in person.

ELI

Thank you your Honor... This keeps getting better and better. Hi... everyone... I'm Eli Eaton and I'm from Pennsylvania and Massachusetts and I'm running for Vice President.

[*a lot more people, lots of tourists, but not as raucous as at the bars and restaurants.*]

CROWD

Cheers.

ELI

What's the one thing on your mind that impacts your daily life that involves the Government?

CROWD 1

Obamacare... it's socialism!

CROWD 2

Yeah, so what... it's working, isn't it? Give up the inflammatory rhetoric already!

ELI

Whoa... let's dial it down a bit... OK, let's not talk about Obamacare per se, let's just talk about health care reform in general. [*approval from crowd.*]   OK... Let me ask a question or two. How many out there have car insurance?

CROWD

Virtually every one applauds.

ELI

OK, now how many people have some form of health care plan, where you pay some amount as a co-pay for medical services or drugs?

CROWD

Some chuckling.

ELI

OK, OK, I mean legal drugs! Hey, we're not in Colorado, here!

CROWD

Applause.

ELI

All of you applauding are   part of a pool used to spread the risk of loss, medical care, etc. among a large number of sick and healthy people... and guess what that means... if you are part of that... then you and everyone else in the pool is, well... a Socialist. [*some boos, but more applause.*] OK, I see some of you are supporting Bernie Sanders! OK, now... how many of you know how much it costs whenever you go see a doctor or go to a hospital?

CROWD

[chanting...]

Bernie... Bernie... Bernie

ELI

OK, OK... Interesting... and how many here go buy a car, an appliance, a home, a plane trip or hire a contractor without knowing how much it costs?

CROWD

[one person.]

Claps and whistles.

ELI

Ladies and gentlemen, there is one of your internet billionaires! He doesn't have to ask what things cost.

CROWD

Laughter.

ELI

Have I made my point? Health care is the only thing in this country that we're all afraid to ask how much it costs, because it's about our bodies... The first thing we need is total transparency in dealing with all aspects of medical care.

CROWD

Applause.

CROWD MEMBER

You're becoming known as a guy who has solutions, so what's your solution for whether Tesla should be allowed to sell its electric cars directly to the customer or be forced to use dealers, like all the other car companies?

ELI

If I'm not mistaken, the Tesla factory is just down the road?

CROWD

Yeah!

ELI

So if I was your usual suck up politician, my answer would be... yes?

[*some crowd acknowledgement.*]

ELI

But I'm not your typical, talking out of both sides of my mouth politician... so thanks for the question... it keeps me focused and you deserve an honest answer, straight and without... excuse my French... any bullshit. This is a tough one, but here goes. [*long pause.*] I don't have a freakin' clue!

CROWD

Surprise, applause, laughter, boos, etc.

ELI

Before you burn me at the stake, remember, I'm not running for President. It won't be my job to propose policies... that's for Congress and the President to do. I'm running to re-define the role of the Vice President as someone who should do more than go to funerals... someone who should be independent and bi-partisan and be empowered by the voters to mediate proposed solutions between the White House and Congress, and be responsible for getting compromises passed and signed into law by the President.

The Vice President should be evaluated on how he is able to get things done. In the Tesla case, we would figure out how this issue fits into our national goals of using less oil in our economy and migrating to clean energy, creating jobs and tech investment and bring the decision makers together and mediate a plan that makes sense, instead of relying on dealer laws that may or may not accomplish what they were supposed to do when enacted almost 100 years ago. We can figure it out, though and make sure everyone's expectations are met, even if it means a change.

CROWD 3
You can't do it alone, so how can one person make a difference?

ELI
Another great question... If I'm elected Vice President, I'll make it a point to hire a truly diverse group for my staffers... Conservatives, Progressives, men, women from all backgrounds, and lifestyles. [*applause and cheering recognizing the lifestyle reference... noteworthy in San Francisco.*] The only common thread will be most of them will be experienced divorce mediators, because that is the specific skill set we'll need to get the Democrats, Republicans and the White House working together. I won't make or propose legislation, but that's how I'll go about getting things done is Washington!

[*some substantial applause and cheering.*]

ELI [CONT'D]
Thank you San Francisco and remember, if you like what you heard here, tell the pollsters and be sure to tell all your friends and family about me and keep asking all the Presidential candidates...

Will you support updating the office of Vice President by naming an independent bi-partisan VeeP if you get the nomination?

[*more substantial applause and cheering, crowd pushing toward Eli asking for autographs, wanting to shake his hand, more selfies, all starting to look like a genuine political rally, but still without the signs, etc.*]

LOCAL TV REPORTER
Can I have a word with you?

ELI
Sure, just let me grab some crab bisque in the sour dough bowl, first.

[*a sign stapled to the booth along with a button worn by the operator reads: We're Eaton for The VeeP.*]

ELI
Thank you. Where did you get the button? I know I never paid for those.

OPERATOR
Oh, I paid 2 bucks for it, over there.

MAYOR YEMANA
Well, wherever there's a void... someone around here is gonna fill it! Here, it would be a crime if you didn't try our coffee.

CUT TO:

16. The Lone Star

[transition video of small chats with people on the Pier, cuts to Facebook, Twitter and You Tube, various signs on restaurants reading... We're Eaton for Vice President, showing significant support being built up around the country.]

[traveling to AZ, NM, NV, UT, ID,CO, KS and then NE, arriving in TX, again showing Welcome to... signs for various states.]

[show Twitter page announcing arrival at Schlitterbahn Water Park near San Antonio, TX, group of people around pool area.]

Schlitterbahn
New Braunfels, TX

ELI

Hi... I'm Eli Eaton... I'm from Pennsylvania and Massachusetts and I'm running for Vice President.

GUEST

So what do you... I mean... where do you stand on immigration?

ELI

Being in Texas, I'm sure that's an important topic... so let's get to it... Let's look at it as a possible three step process... first we have to stem the flow of illegal immigration into the U.S., second... we have to have Congress decide what is in the national interest regarding the 10-12 million illegal residents we now have and third, how can we integrate the illegal residents into a more meaningful type of legal status.

Let's take it one step at a time. First, how can we stem the flow of illegal immigrants into the U.S.? We have to understand why they come in the first place. If we know the reason they come, then we can find a way to deal with it. Let me ask, why do they come across the border?

GUEST 1

To find work, to be with family.

GUEST 2

To be part of the American dream, to be in the land of opportunity.

GUEST 3
To have hope for your family.

ELI
OK... OK... that's a good start.. let's look at that. So, if those things were only available in the U.S., no wall or border will be able to keep someone out, because the incentive is too great. It's like water flowing into your basement. You've got to divert it at the source, not just patch up cracks in the foundation. If Congress really wants to stem the illegal immigration, then they have to work with the foreign governments to create those opportunities, there, like the auto factories being built in Mexico... more like that. I don't think the long term solution rests with border police. The next question is how to integrate the 10 to 12 million currently in this country. Let me ask a question... how many of you fly on one of the airlines?

[several respond with applause.]

ELI [CON'TD]
OK, how many are familiar with customer loyalty programs, you know with the discount cards, at supermarkets, etc.?

[more respond with applause.]

ELI [CON'TD]
OK... so many of you are willing to belong to a club or organization that has several levels of membership, like American Airlines in Dallas... where the more miles you fly, the more benefits you get, like getting better seats on the plane and deals on special promotions... so it makes sense to me that we could initially create levels of residency or pre-citizenship.

Most every publicly owned corporation in this country has more than one type of shareholder... common and preferred shareholders.

We don't view the differences as being inferior, or second class... we just view them as being different, with different rights and responsibilities. If Congress votes to integrate the illegal immigrants by some form of path to legality, each effected person could choose what type of... or level of legality works best for them and at least everyone would be integrated, each with different rights and responsibilities.

*[people are taking pictures, videos on
their cell phones, asking Eli to take
pictures with them.]*

GUEST
Eli... would you be able to visit with a group of friends with this problem?

ELI
Love to... but first I really want to take a ride on the Master Blaster... it looks like a real hoot!

17. Helen of Troy

[transition showing maps, path along IA, NE, AR, LA, MO, MS, TN, etc.]

[and arriving at Troy State University in Troy, AL.]

ELI
Hi... I'm Eli Eaton... I'm from Pennsylvania and Massachusetts and I'm running for Vice President.

HELEN
I don't know... can we trust someone who's not a redneck?

ELI

Well, I once held a business lunch at a vending machine... and according to Jeff Foxworthy, I just might be a redneck!... but I did live in Atlanta for awhile... went to school at Emory.

DAVID

OK, we'll be the judge of that... so if you get elected, you gonna take our guns away from us?

ELI

OK... I'll take that as a question about the Second Amendment! First, before we get started, I own several guns and I certainly feel safer at night knowing it's near my bed.. just in case.

STUDENTS
All rights!

ELI

Anyway... there's been a lot of emotional rhetoric about 'gun control' especially since the tragedies at Aurora, Newtown and Oregon. First, the 2nd Amendment was part of the bill of rights passed in 1789, when there were only a few million people in this country. Now there are well over 325 million... big difference. Second, the right to bear arms was to protect against any invader. Back then, all anyone had were cannons, muskets and pistols, so it made sense to protect the right to have the same weapons in the hands of the people. Today, I hope no one seriously wants to allow people to keep and bear... oh, say... nuclear weapons, ICBM's and cruise missiles.

FRED
Yeah... I'll take a couple!

ELI

Yeah... just what we need... you and Kim, a couple of twenty year olds.. toe to toe with nukes.

FRED

Nuke the commie!

ELI

OK...OK... settle down... I think we only need to get him a better haircut!

STUDENTS

Laughter.

ELI

I would support Congress to re-write the second amendment to re-affirm the people's right to bear arms... but only those that are necessary for protection against what is available to criminals, home invaders and the such, but also implement a system to manage the arms out there so that they are not used for harming or threatening others beyond the intent of the 2nd amendment.

JEANE

Eli... would you be able to do an interview with the campus radio station?

ELI

Would love to... but first let me go to the caf... for some crawfish and hushpuppies.

18. The Fuse

[*transition thru maps... GA, FL, SC, NC and arriving at Carl's Ice Cream in Fredericksburg, VA.*]

[*several small groups hanging around all eating ice cream, talking with Eli and his son Matt, who has joined him during summer break.*]

ELI

Hi... I'm Eli Eaton... and I'm running for Vice President. What's the most important issue to you?

PATRON

Right to life. Family values. I pray every night for the souls of those poor unborn babies killed.

[in a serious tone.]

ELI

Well, I can see that this is a really important issue for you... do you have a few moments so I can tell you where I'm coming from?

PATRON
Sure.

ELI

I think this issue best exemplifies many of the problems we have in this country.   People feel passionately about something and draw a line in the sand and refuse to hear the other person's point of view... that's why Congress ends up in gridlock, nobody wants to negotiate or compromise. Let me ask you... about half of the country agrees with you and about half disagrees. Are you OK with that?

PATRON
No sir... I'm not, until every last soul is saved.

ELI

I admire your passion... I truly do. Can you see that there's someone in Congress who feels just as passionately as you do about the right of a woman to choose what happens to her own body... and both of you refuse to compromise... and that's how Congress ends up gridlocked... can't get anything done?

PATRON
I don't care.

ELI

Well, most politicians would walk away from you at this point, but I'd like to share with you how we might handle this situation.. would that be OK?

PATRON
OK.

ELI

I'm not going to take sides, I am a proud and loyal American... I obey the laws and rulings of this country... and right now, agree or not, there is a Supreme Court ruling which unfortunately disagrees with your belief... that's Roe v. Wade. Because that is the law of the land, like it or not, I feel compelled to follow it. Now I support you in every way, any legal attempt to change that law. The key here is education.

If I am elected Vice President we should make sure Congress passes a budget including substantial sums of money which would be used by those who disagree with that law, to try to educate the others about your view of right to life... but it has to be done in a civilized manner. If you look at how in one generation, we have turned smoking around 180 degrees in this country... think what education can do about any issue, even yours? Believe it or not, education is the key, and if it's meant to be, things will change and I do support allocating money for that education.

I hope you'll ask every candidate for President, if they will support nominating an independent bi-partisan Vice President if nominated.

LOCAL TV REPORTER
Do you have time for an interview?

ELI
Sure thing, just let my try one of those vanilla cones.

CUT TO:

MINI-MART IN FREDERICKSBURG:

[*Eli and Matt are getting gas at the Central Park area, a guy wearing a Tom Brady jersey is in the background filling up a flat tire, when they encounter three middle eastern type young men in the convenience store, dealing with the clerk. Eli and Matt are behind them and a biker type with pony-tail. **It is the morning of July 4th**.*]

[*to the three young men.*]

FEMALE CLERK
Here's your change for 10 gallons of gasoline, use pump 9.

[*in a combination British/Arabic
accent, holding out the change for
another purchase.*]

YOUNG MAN
I would like a pack of fags.

FEMALE CLERK
Excuse me?

[*immediately jumping in punching his
friend on the upper ar*m.]

SECOND YOUNG MAN
A pack of cigarettes.

FEMALE CLERK
aah....what brand?

YOUNG MAN
It doesn't matter.

[*briefly taking in the whole situation.*]

FEMALE CLERK
I'll need to see some ID.

[*now somewhat belligerently.*]

YOUNG MAN
I don't need any ID.

FEMALE CLERK
If there's any question, I need to check IDs, it's the law.

[*getting more agitated.*]

YOUNG MAN
I don't need a whole pack, just give me one.

FEMALE CLERK
It's against the law to sell single cigarettes.

YOUNG MAN
You and your laws...You're just making me trouble because we're Muslims. Just give me one cigarette, woman.

BIKER
Here, pal... here's a cigarette.

YOUNG MAN
Thank you... at least you are honorable.

[*he takes the cigarette and holds it somewhat awkwardly out in front of himself staring at it as he and his friends exit the store, everyone in the area look at each other as if an uncomfortable situation was just averted.*]

CUT TO:
[as *Eli and Matt are getting into their car, an old black pickup truck leaves the station squealing tires loudly.*]

ELI
Do you smell fertilizer?

MATT
You're just smelling burning rubber.

ELI
What about that whole thing isn't right?

CUT TO:

INSIDE OF CAR:

MATT
What, those guys?

ELI
Yeah...

MATT
What do you think, they're terrorists, just because they're Muslims. It was probably some truth or dare thing smoking their first cigarette. Stop being so FBI.

ELI
I don't know... it's July 4th, I feel like a hot dog.

MATT
Roger that.

CUT TO:

[*Matt is driving, Eli in the passenger seat, it is July 4th. They spot the pickup truck that screamed out of the gas station being driven by the middle-eastern type young men they just encountered at the gas station.*]

ELI
Aren't those the guys we just saw?

[*pointing to the truck passing them.*]

MATT
Yeah... so?

ELI

What's wrong with that picture?

MATT

Oh, please don't tell me you're gonna go FBI on me again. [*Pause*] What... you really think they're terrorists... just because they look middle eastern?

ELI

That... and a tarp covered pickup truck filled with trash barrels, gasoline containers, Alabama plates, no name in the truck, wires hanging out the back... smell of fertilizer... yeah, the whole picture.

MATT

Seriously? I thought you raised me better than being so judgmental... are we profiling here?

ELI

... and what if it turns out they are carrying bombs to a July 4th event... and the cigarette is for a delayed fuse... like in the movies?

MATT

... or just trucking in some ribs and southern bar b q to a July 4th picnic?

ELI

That's my point... we don't know... [*pondering*] interesting dilemma, should it be our call or should we just let someone know about it.

MATT

Geez, you really want to create a society of... report your neighbor... sounds like Nazi Germany.

ELI

Except they're not our neighbors. And if they were a legitimate business, they'd have a business name on the truck for advertising.

MATT

So just because they can't afford a fancy new truck, they're terrorists?

ELI

I don't know... and neither do you... if we see something that looks out of place... don't we have a moral obligation to at least let someone know?

MATT

Sounds like a huge price to pay, everyone spying on each other.

ELI

I sure hope you're right...   but what if we saw those Russian brothers acting weird before the finish line at the Boston Marathon?

[*Matt shrugs, Eli turns on the radio.*]

ELI

This is killin me...I've got to let someone know about that truck.

[*takes out his cell phone and starts dialing 911.*]

MATT

Are you sure this is the right thing to do?

ELI

Yes... better safe than sorry. Sometimes you just gotta go with your gut. This just doesn't feel right.

[*no dialogue transition, Eli is talking on cell phone as car is traveling, music in background, then...*]

ELI (CONT'D)

... just thought I should let the authorities know. Yes, my name is Eli Eaton... no... I'm quite serious... yeah...I'm driving a lot around the country running a grass roots campaign for Vice President... yeah... yeah... ok, bye.

ELI [CONT'D]

That was a waste... she sounded as if she could care less... that's going nowhere... and she has no clue who I am, either... naturally!

MATT

Get used to nobody knowing you... especially if you ever actually get to be Vice President. Anyway, let it go... odds are nothing is going to happen.

ELI

I just can't shake it... what was the name of that cop we met this morning at breakfast?

MATT

Hank Woje...something. Here's his card... Fredericksburg Police Department.

ELI
Here, let me try him.

[*Eli dials and starts talking on the phone.*]

Hey, Hank, this is Eli Eaton, we met at breakfast... yeah, well something weird happened after we met this morning...

CUT TO:

19. It's the Bomb

[a bit later, they stop at a local BBQ joint.]

[BBQ restaurant, Eli and Matt are sitting, TV is on in background while Eli is talking with patrons about running for VP.]

[on the TV in the background, there is a 240th 4th of July festival taking place with lots of white tarp tents in a few aisles all on a field containing food vendors, craft booths and 1776 re-enactment activities going on along with an interview of Gov. Barrett, before she joins the parade.]

ON A TV:

TV ANNOUNCER 1

so... Governor Barrett, we really appreciate you campaigning at our July 4th festival... it's nice to have a Presidential candidate visit Fredericksburg... and one last question before going over to the parade... if you do get the Republican nomination, and Laurie Plimpton gets the Democratic nod, we will then be assured of our first female President... do you think we as a nation are ready for that?

ANN

Oh... absolutely! But don't compare me with the tax and spend, e-mail deleting, liberal socialist Laurie Plimpton... we have very different ways on how to move our country forward... [*under female leadership.*]

[***as she says the word 'forward', a bomb explodes*** *in the background of the interview, the TV camera shakes violently, everyone on camera flinches and protecting themselves by pulling their arms over their heads, as screaming erupts and both cameras from the TV station and Emily and Dave's jerk around trying to get a shot of the scene as a large billow of a mushroom cloud fire and smoke rises and they both start moving the equipment   to the scene with cameras rolling, jerking around.*]

PATRON
Turn that up!

CLOSE IN ON TV MONITOR:

TV ANNOUNCER 1

An explosion has just gone off behind us... we're trying to get to get over there... there's screaming... people are running away... I see some EMTs and firefighters already racing to the scene as others are leaving... sirens are going off... already a couple ambulances are arriving... I see a few people on the ground... I can't tell if anyone is seriously hurt... or dead, there is already a ring of first responders at the scene... we can't tell what's going on...

[*shoving a microphone in the face of an EMT.*]

Can you tell us what is going on?!?

EMT

Please stay back... we don't know exactly what we have here.

TV ANNOUNCER 1

It looks like there are about five or so people down... they are all moving... being triaged... I don't see anyone motionless... thank God...

EMT

You're going to have to leave the area... there are ambulances arriving...

TV ANNOUNCER 1

We're going to let the first responders do their jobs... I've been informed there are no deaths and six people injured... nobody appears to be critical... I've just been informed the police have stopped three middle eastern males over there... Nick... let's get the crew over there and see what's going on...

ON ANOTHER TV MONITOR:

TV ANNOUNCER 2
We are receiving multiple Twitter feeds and Facebook posts indicating an explosion has just taken place at the July 4th parade... several people are reported down... fire and EMT responders are arriving at the scene as we speak... please be aware, we have not received any official confirmation as yet, but our mobile crew is there and we expect some form of confirmation in just a matter of seconds... we have Bob St. Clair on the scene... Bob... what can you tell us.

TV ANNOUNCER 1
Jane, we were covering the July 4th parade at the festival and then responded to a police BOLO, a be on the lookout for a group of young men driving an old black pickup truck... just when we saw police approach what appeared to be the truck in question... about fifty yards away from our position along the parade route, an explosion erupted in the truck, about a thirty yards from the reviewing stand... there's still a large cloud of smoke billowing up into the sky... people are screaming... there appears to be a handful of people down... I can't be sure of their condition... we should be there momentarily... EMT and fire responders are already there... I hear sirens from what I assume are ambulances arriving at the scene... there's a lot of chaos.. a lot of people are leaving the area... others are rushing to the scene of the explosion...

CUT TO:
TV NEWS INTERVIEW:

[*later.*]

TV REPORTER

I have Fredericksburg police officer, Henry Wojehowitz, who was one of the first responders at the explosion earlier and the arresting officer... how were you able to respond so quickly to the explosion and apprehend the suspects at the scene?

WOJEHOWITZ

I was assigned as security for the July 4th festival and received a tip about three young middle eastern males in a pickup truck behaving suspiciously... it was only a matter of minutes when I noticed a pickup truck matching the description with the three terrorists parked over on the east side along the parade route. I notified command and advised our T1 protocol be activated.

TV REPORTER
... and what is a T1 protocol?

WOJEHOWITZ

That's when a credible imminent terrorist threat is ascertained, all available local resources are mobilized and ready to respond... SWAT, medical, containment...

TV REPORTER
...and then what happened?

WOJEHOWITZ

I yelled for everyone to immediately evacuate the area, and about 60 seconds later, the bed of the pickup truck exploded. Apparently the explosion was premature because the three male terrorists were still hanging around the area about 30-40 yards away, and appeared stunned by the explosion.

I immediately drew my weapon and contained them with the help of a couple guys in the area. Fortunately, the EMTs were already mobilized and they were able to start treating victims.

TV REPORTER

Officer Wojehowitz, you are a real hero... thank you so much. The people of Fredericksburg are proud of your valor.

WOJEHOWITZ

[*modestly.*] Really, I was just doing my job... the real hero is the guy who gave me the tip. He saved countless lives today... I would never have been in the area otherwise... all I did was...

FADE OUT:

FADE IN:

DINER RESTAURANT:

[*noticing Eli's car in front of the restaurant with the "Eli Eaton for VeeP" on the sides and looking for a local story, dressed in a sport coat with a TV4 microphone.*]

LOCAL TV REPORTER

You wouldn't happen to be Eli Eaton, would you?

ELI
Yes, I am. This is my son, Matt.

LOCAL TV REPORTER
My producer back in the newsroom says there is an unconfirmed report that you were the one who reported the truck involved with the bombing at the Fredericksburg Fourth of July Festival earlier today. Can you confirm that for me?

[*obviously shaken up at hearing the news of a possible connection.*]

ELI
Really? I did report an unusual truck earlier this morning, but I have no idea if it was involved with...

LOCAL TV REPORTER
The alleged vehicle in question was a black old model pickup truck with Alabama plates. Is that the one you reported?

ELI
Actually, yeah... that's the one.

LOCAL TV REPORTER
Would you agree to an interview? It looks like no one was killed at the festival, but several were seriously injured... and without your report, and the police intervention, there certainly would have been deaths involved, possibly Gov. Ann Barrett who was there campaigning for President. Mr. Eaton, you're a patriot... a real hero!

[*later, at the end of the interview.*]

*[shots of social media erupting with
the news of the explosion and Eli's
involvement.]*

*[local TV reporter listening to a cell
phone in one ear and handing it to
Eli.]*

ELI
Yes... this is Eli Eaton.

VOICE ON CELL PHONE
...one moment, please... the producer at Face the Press wants
to speak with you, are you available to be on the show
Sunday?

ELI
Aaah, sure... we're only a day away.

CUT TO:
SHOT OF: **DARK COMPUTER SCREEN**
*[screen shows a conversation taking
place like texting, with hundreds of
blinking internet computer LEDs in the
background.]*

COMPUTER SCREEN

Daily 10 items for broad dissemination over internet

1. Puppy surprised by bird landing on head.
2. Guy running for VP alerts police on terror
    bombing.
Is this guy 4 real?
Getting lot of YT uploads mult OPs
FB up

T up.
Seems 2 b real deal.
ck YT
[pause]
interesting
want 2 c if he got game.
K

Go for viral. Done.

CUT TO:

[*video montage of...*
1,000,000+ emails   and push notices all of the sudden sent
out in a matter of seconds to news rooms, a la scenes from
Citizen Kane,   media centers, web site addresses sent, links
to You Tube, Facebook and Twitter. traditional media now
picking up on it.]

[*montage of newsrooms asking about Eli Eaton, checking*
him out, editors telling reporters to go find him and see
what's this all about... **Who is Eli Eaton?**... *and why is he*
trending on Twitter. Checking You Tube uploads, Facebook
search show hundreds of upload to personal pages, cut to FB
page for Eli, Twitter account and You Tube channel. Matt
has left for home.]

TRANSITION BACK TO:

SECOND SCENE:

FACE THE PRESS:

20. A Bite Out of The Big Apple

FACE THE PRESS STUDIO SET:

CONTINUED FROM SECOND SCENE:

JULY 10, 2016

RUDD [CONT'D]
... Good morning, we start off this Sunday... with our thoughts and prayers to those injured in the Fredericksburg bombing on Monday. Reports on that later. First, the man being credited with saving numerous lives and injuries last Monday in Fredericksburg. It has been going viral all week on social media, but If you haven't been paying attention, you've probably never heard of, Eli Eaton, who is running for national office... watch.

[*shows montage of quick series of You
Tube videos of Eli talking in various
restaurants showing growing crowds
of patrons around him and leading up
to clips of the bombing in
Fredericksburg last Monday.*]

CUT BACK TO:

GREEN ROOM:

[*interview showing on monitor in
green room, in the background.*]

RUSS

Governor, they want to cover the gun control issue with you and your reaction to the bombing last week. We're still riding a huge wave of public sympathy for you and even more now, after Monday... this is your moment. We need to score big this morning to get the uncommitted delegates in our camp before the convention next week. Are you clear on how you need to come across this morning?

ANN

I know, I know... the traditional conservative family values wife who tragically loses her husband to gun violence, who still believes in the right to bear arms and more homeland security after the bombing last Monday...

RUSS

That's good, but after Monday, you've got to show some flexibility on the gun issue, but don't go beyond national registration... you won't lose points on that one... and don't suggest in any way you were hurt in the bombing, we don't need another Brian Williams situation.

CUT BACK TO:

STUDIO INTERVIEW SET:

RUDD
Good morning, Eli.

ELI
Good morning, Mike.

RUDD

It is nothing short of remarkable what has happened to you over the past few months, even the past few days, but I understand that you have actually been campaigning since last fall.

ELI

That's right... I've got a lot of ground to cover.

RUDD

Let's be clear from the outset. Are you running for President as an Independent?

CUT TO:

GREEN ROOM ON TV MONITOR:

ELI

Ah... no, Mike... I'm actually running for... Vice President.

[*taken back from that disclosure.*]

ANN

What the hell did he just say?

RUSS

Ssssh.

CLOSE IN ON:

GREEN ROOM MONITOR:

RUDD

I don't recollect anyone actually ever openly running for Vice President, I mean, the Vice President is always selected by the Presidential nominee... so just how does one officially, that is, publically run for Vice President?

ELI

Well, Mike... for the past 10 months, I've been driving across the country, visiting... talking... eating and mostly listening... and there are a lot of people out there... fed up with the gridlock and partisan posturing in Washington... the bickering... between the Democrats and the Republicans. That's why Trump and Carson's numbers were so high right out of the gate last fall in the early polls. To use a family analogy, it's like two kids whining all the time at each other... and frankly, people are fed up listening to it and all. I think any parent knows exactly what I'm talking about.

RUDD

As a parent, I totally get it, but logistically, just how does someone run for Vice President? There is no constitutional precedent.

ELI

I'm getting the people behind me... the voters... both the Democrats and Republicans... common sense doesn't belong to any one party, Mike. Hopefully, my support will be bi-partisan and so strong, that both the Democratic and Republican nominees... whomever they may be, will have no choice but to pick me... or risk losing the general election in November. It's 2016 and the people should have some say on who gets selected to run for Vice President. It's time we update the office of Vice President after 227 years, with a real job description and real responsibilities, no matter who ends up in the White House.

CUT BACK TO STUDIO:

RUDD

Two months ago, I would have dismissed you as tilting at windmills... without a prayer of being successful... but I have to admit... given the totally unpredictable current election cycle and the influence of our social media these days... I'm not sure what is possible any more. Some of your recent You Tube videos have had tens of millions of hits.

ELI

That's what they tell me. Listen... we're talking 2016 here. The Vice President has to do more than go to funerals and walk around on a short Presidential leash with the Senate gavel stuck up his butt!

[Rudd flinches at Eli's forthright language]

ELI [CONT'D]

Listen, President Obama was right, during his last State of the Union speech when he said... "We need to change the system, to reflect our better selves."

It's high time we change the office of the Vice President to actually **doooo** something for the country, as an independent liaison, working between the White House and Congress. That one step can change the system of partisan politics, which has driven us to become our lesser selves. We can be better... all of us.

RUDD

But what can you realistically do? There's no constitutional VP job description... the VP ends up doing whatever the President wants, so why shouldn't he... or she get to pick the Vice President?

ELI

I agree the President should have a high level political ally to help accomplish his or her agenda, but... that position should be hand-picked by POTUS like the President's Chief of Staff, or it could be something new like the Assistant to the President... AP, for short. A perfect example would be if Laurie Plimpton gets elected, she could pick her brother as a former President as her AP and he could act as her highest and closest official advisor, like the VP has done, recently, like Joe Biden for President Obama or Dick Cheney for President Bush.

The selection of the nominee for Vice President on the other hand, as a constitutional position, should be the result of a public process and the VP should be responsible for managing things between Congress and the White House, independent of either branch of government.

RUDD

But isn't it totally up to the President... what the Vice President is responsible for, except for overseeing the Senate?

ELI

Actually, except for the Senate part, and the Electoral College thing, there's no constitutional job description for anything else for the Vice President. In 1804, after the 12th Amendment, the Executive branch took control of the VP and no one has questioned that since... until now. But constitutionally, the VP isn't tied to the President at all. Many scholars question which branch of government the office of Vice President belongs in...

I'm making the case that if the Constitution doesn't explicitly put the Vice President in any specific branch of government, then it should be independent of either branch.

Besides, the Executive Branch is strong enough these days on its own... it doesn't need the VP as one more cheerleader for the President.

CUT TO **GREEN ROOM:**

[*interview continues on the TV screen.*]

RUSS
Are you getting this?

ANN
This guy is taking up all my time.

ELI [CONT'D]
... and here's something the conservative constitutional strict constructionists and originalists should love... remember, back with the original Constitution, the Vice President was the Presidential candidate who came in second! They intended that the Vice President would be a political adversary of the President, most likely from a different party, so there would be yet another check and balance on the Executive branch. It's time we go back to a model like that, and that's why I'm bringing the VeeP issue to the table in 2016.

RUDD
What you're proposing is a total paradigm shift and I'm not sure if your vision is... delusional pipedream... or pure genius.

ELI
Well, given your two options... I can live with genius! And the best part... it's totally constitutional.

CUT TO:

STUDIO:

[*Emily nudging Dave to focus on Eli
while the interview continues, muted.*]

[*whispering to Emily, she nods.*]

DAVE
I think he just won the 20 bucks.

CUT TO:
GREEN ROOM:

[*running his hands through his hair
recognizing the radical potential of
what's being proposed by Eli.*]

RUSS
Holy crap!

ANN
What's this guy doing?

RUSS
He's doing what we should be doing... if you really want to
end up being the Vice President.

CUT TO:
FTP INTERVIEW SET:

RUDD
I understand you have a lot of inside out 760° views on the
hot button issues that have been getting lots of attention on
social media, so let's see what you're putting on the table,
then we'll talk about what led up to Monday's bombing in
Fredericksburg.

ELI

Let's do it. But remember, I'm not advocating any policy, per se... I'm just using various policy issues as an example of how I would act as an independent liaison between the White House and Congress, not advocating for this or that policy.

RUDD

OK... I get that, but it would be instructive to see where you're coming from to understand what an 'Independent' liaison stands for. Given the ongoing threats we have to our national security, after events like Paris and San Bernadino, what can we do to promote safety and security in this country.

ELI

First, we have to be smart about what is going on. Bombastic rhetoric isn't going to make us safe and secure. I would hope that we as a society know that talking and acting tough like a bully doesn't get the job done. We are in a war of ideology, not of territory. Tanks, bombers, ground troops are NOT the answer and in fact, only exacerbate the problem. We've got to be smart.

RUDD

OK then, but if you want to be seen as someone different, you need to provide specifics, not just generalized comments.

ELI

Great, so let's get specific. Let me ask you, what western democracy has had a history of small group ideological terrorist bombings in restaurants, public transportation and shopping malls?

RUDD
That would be Israel.

ELI

Exactly... and how much terrorist activity have we heard lately in Israel? Not nearly as much as in the past, right?

RUDD

Clearly, much less... only on rare occasions, now.

ELI

Bingo... so if we want to figure out what we could and should do to lessen small group and lone wolf terrorist activity... Who you gonna call? Ghostbusters? No, we should be learning from their experience, and Israel has that proven experience.

RUDD

So what have they done, that we might adopt?

ELI

First, they are very good at profiling... and no... profiling doesn't have to be a dirty word. Instead of arming police with armored tanks and military style equipment, we should have smart people on the streets, in restaurants, in shopping malls and on public transportation... who are trained to detect terrorist behavior and stop it before it is able to cause any harm. That's one smart way to effectively mobilize our resources to address the problem.

Second, they have an interesting policy. They will try to destroy the home of any terrorist, which means the entire family of the terrorist will lose their home if anyone in the family engages in any terrorist activity... and guess what that does?

It makes everyone in that family own up and be responsible for any terrorist activity within the household of their family... and once that family knows it will lose its home if anyone of them becomes a terrorist, it will make the family stop it before it gets off the ground... and that policy may just have inhibited the situation in San Bernadino, since the parents lived with terrorists in the same house. And yeah, I know we'll have to find a way to do it constitutionally.

Remember, the threat from ISIS is not a massive invasion on our shores of terrorists, it is from individual and small groups becoming radicalized and acting out of ideology and attempts to string together small terrorist events to create a state of fear in this country. We must learn from Israel, how to effectively deal with that type of threat to our national security and safety. It's just the smart way to address this challenge.

RUDD
OK, let's shift gears and look at the hot political issue after the passing of Supreme Court Justice Scalia. Where do you stand on the political divide between President Obama nominating a replacement Justice and the Senate Republicans who steadfastly maintain that the nomination should be deferred to the next President. Where do you come down on this issue?

ELI
Great question... and this issue really highlights the purpose why I am running for Vice President as a bi-partisan candidate. First, both the President and the Senators, swore an oath to support and defend the Constitution, so clearly the President has a sworn duty to nominate a new Justice, while the Senators have the same sworn duty to execute their responsibilities to at least take action and vote on any nominee.

This is going to sound a bit radical, but using my 760° method of problem analysis... you know, if I was the Vice President, as Chair of the Senate... I would lock up and sequester every member of the Judiciary Committee in a big conference room, I think there are around 20 of them... and not let them out until they exercised their Constitutional 'advise and consent' responsibility by recommending at least three candidates for the President to consider and agreed to by at least 16 of the Senators, or roughly 80%... and there is a plume of white smoke rising from the chimney in the room.

I would then strongly urge the President to put aside his personal political agenda and nominate one of those candidates in an effort to depoliticize the process of nominating a new Justice during the final year of a Presidency. It's the right thing to do for the country, to have political diversity on the Court and to find a moderate Justice to act as the swing vote on the very challenging cases before the court. Also, it's all about the math. There's only a 50/50 chance the President's party will win the White House in November, while there is a better than 50/50 chance the other Party will still be the majority in the Senate.

It just makes logical sense for both parties to compromise and get a known commodity, given the uncertainty of the November election outcome and it would go a long way to demonstrate to the people that the two branches of government can actually function without all the political histrionics of the past decade. Both sides have to look at this issue from both the inside out and the outside in... my 760° method of resolving tough challenges.

Listen, bottom line... I use the family analogy a lot and this is no different. It's like having two petulant children fighting over what movie to go see as a family.

As the parent, you just put them in a room and wait for them to work it out, or they just end up stewing in the room and do nothing. Most of the time, they will eventually agree.

RUDD

OK, interesting approach, as a parent, I get it... maybe we can also learn something from the College of Cardinals... and I'd love to be a fly on the wall in the room of that one with Senator Cruz and Senator Franken mano a mano, but let's move on and get to economics...to taxes... nobody likes them... but as Justice Holmes stated... "It's the cost of a civilized society."

However, the major gripes heard today are all about fairness, the top 1% versus the 99%, middle America, paying one's fair share... loopholes... special interests, lobbyists and income inequities, tithing, flat tax rates.
The Presidential debates have all allowed the candidates to speak out on taxes, for the record...what do you make of it all?

ELI

Fairness is indeed the key. I believe the current tax system is just too damn complex to be fair. Heck, even the IRS gets into trouble because it doesn't even know it's own laws! 501 [c] [4] this... 1231 [b] [3] little i that... give me a break. Here's a picture of the current federal tax laws stacked up end to end.

[*shows picture stacked tax books to camera.*]

Mike, I'm 6'3"... that's just wrong, plain and simple [*pointing emphatically at the picture...*]

RUDD

Not many would argue with that, but what is the solution?

ELI

Well, Congress needs to make it stupid simple to raise the money needed to operate our government.

It has to be non-political, pure basic public finance, not using politics to favor this group or that group with tax savings, something even I can understand... like here, I'm buying a car... add a tax on top of that and boom... done. No tax returns, no April 15th... and no paying my C.P.A. hundreds of bucks to do my taxes.

Specifically, we need to have a debate on whether we should collect taxes on what we contribute to society with our wages and hard work, or on what we buy... and take out of society and keep for ourselves. Personally, I think the latter is easier and better meets our national goals and makes more sense with today's population and in our economy.

RUDD

So are you advocating scrapping the entire income tax system?

ELI
No No.

CUT TO:
GREEN ROOM:

[Ann and Russ are intently watching.]

ELI [CONT'D]

A solution worth exploring is eliminating most of the income tax on salaries and wages... for individuals and... make up the lost revenue by implementing a national sales tax based upon stated national goals and eliminating all deductions. A hybrid tax system... kinda like the Toyota Prius of tax laws.

RUDD

Many would say that a national sales tax is not fair for the majority of low income families.

ELI

There you go, with the fairness thing again. You're trying to politicize it... can't do that. We should collect taxes based on stated national goals and objectives... not on what's fair for that group or who should pay this tax or get that deduction. Then, the whole problem of fairness would be eliminated.

RUDD

The devil must be in the details.

ELI

First, it is absolutely ludicrous that Congress doesn't establish in writing, it's goals and objectives for each Congress. I don't know of any business in the country worth its salt that doesn't have a written list of goal and objectives to measure it's performance over time.

So, let's say that we can pressure Congress to establish the national goals of creating and maintaining high levels of good jobs and low unemployment... along with preserving the future of the Social Security system for retirees, reducing illegal immigration, reducing our use of oil, promoting clean energy, reducing the trade deficit and reducing welfare.

Any argument on those goals? Democratic or Republican?
Any of you guys behind the cameras got a problem with any
of that?

[*soft negative shake of the camera.*]

RUDD
I would hope not.

ELI
Good, then If there was no income tax on most wages, more
people would be encouraged to work.   That means less
people on welfare, more people would be paying into FICA
and that helps the Social Security system. Most Americans
would then not even have to file tax returns... and that would
free up the IRS from hassling honest hard working
Americans... and 501 [c] [4] organizations and improve the
public's attitudes toward government.

RUDD
And what about the fairness of a national sales tax, taxing
food and clothing?

ELI
First, all Congress needs to do is exempt those items
necessary for a basic acceptable living standard here in the
U.S. like food,   necessary clothing, medical needs, basic
transportation, etc.
Second, while the IRS checks businesses to make sure the
sales tax is collected, they can also check on illegal workers,
which helps the immigration issue. Any tax law stacked up
against clearly stated national goals by definition will be fair.

RUDD
For example?

ELI
If we want to insure all **LEGAL** American citizens... have a minimum quality of life, including basic food, clothing, medical care and transportation, we can simply exempt those things from the sales tax, like many states now do already.

Let's use cars for example. We can exempt from the sales tax, the most fuel efficient cars designed and manufactured by American workers and impose the highest sales tax on the highest fuel consumption cars made with no American workers and watch how many fuel efficient American built cars are sold! Next thing you know, even more jobs and many of our national priorities will be less of a problem.

RUDD
Well, let's explore another area... former Governor Barrett will be joining us later and I'm sure the issue of gun control will come up... what is your approach to the emotional issue of gun control in light of Newtown, Aurora, Charleston and Oregon?

CUT TO:

GREEN ROOM:

[*sarcastically, pulls out pad to take notes, Ann glued to monitor, speechless.*]

RUSS
This should be good.

ELI

I think we do America a disservice to frame the debate as gun control. What it really should be... is a discussion on how to effectively manage the Second Amendment... as it relates to the very real problem we have with gun violence in this country, especially in the hands of mentally challenged persons.

CUT TO:
DAVE'S CAMERA MONITOR:

ELI [CONT'D]

Listen, the Second Amendment was enacted over 200 years ago and it specifically refers to the need of a well regulated Militia. Well, back in the 1790'S that was necessary. Over the past 200 years we have delegated that responsibility to local, county and state police departments... and obviously, they bear arms. Back then, all they had were flintlocks, muskets and cannons...so the individual's right to bear those same arms kept any threat at bay. Makes sense.

CUT TO:

GREEN ROOM MONITOR:

ELI [CONT'D]

Fast forward to today, I hope the NRA isn't advocating that an individual has the Second Amendment right to keep and bear nuclear weapons, cruise missiles and the like. But... I think the Second Amendment is still relevant.

Local police just can't protect the individual against all harm... specifically gangs, home invaders, local crime and the such. The Second Amendment guarantees individuals the right to own guns for self protection and that is and should always be sacrosanct.

Second, is the emotional part... and here I speak from personal experience. I have lived alone and frankly, I feel a lot safer and sleep better at night, knowing that I have a semi-automatic pistol near my bed which can be loaded, chambered and safety off within a matter of seconds.

RUSS
Crap... this guy's good.

CUT TO:
CLOCK SHOWING TIME ELAPSED:

CUT BACK TO:
INTERVIEW SET:

ELI [CON'TD]
We need to update the Second Amendment to reflect the reality of today... we must unconditionally recognize and guarantee the individual's right to keep arms, but... and here's the but... that right comes with necessary management of that constitutional right so we can do something to avoid any further tragedies like Newtown, Aurora and Oregon .
As we know, any constitutional right, even free speech, is not absolute. I don't think I could look into a Newtown parent's face, and not do something... to stem gun violence. That was... and still is, just too horrible... and not the future I want for America.

CUT TO:
CLOCK SHOWING EVEN MORE TIME ELAPSED:

CUT TO:
GREEN ROOM MONITOR:

[*Russ glances at his watch nodding head back and forth projecting time.*]

ANN

What's going on here? Have you seen the time? That bastard is going to bump me! I'm not going to get on, am I?

CUT TO:

INTERVIEW SET:

RUDD

I'm sure there will be much more discussion on that, but let's move on... what's your approach to the deficit and the economics of government spending?

CUT TO:
CLOCK SHOWS SEGMENT IS COMING TO END:

CUT TO GREEN ROOM:

[*Ann begins to gather up her coat and briefcase, really pissed off, Russ has her hold off momentarily.*]
FOCUS ON MONITOR:

RUDD

We haven't much time remaining, and we've not even touched on other key issues like health care and immigration. Can you give us a quick overview of how health care fits into your vision for America?

RUSS
That's it... We're toast!

[*Ann leaves room in a huff, heads to ladies room.*]

CUT TO:

INTERVIEW SET:

[*Emily puts her hand on Dave's shoulder, pointing to the set, pleased watching Eli all this time. Her gaze sharpens...she can't wait to debate him... to change his position to a more left orientation on gun control, profiling and immigration. Emily feels compromised and frustrated having to work for Ann for the money, but at least she's in the political mix.*]

EMILY

This is great!

CUT TO:
GREEN ROOM

[*Russ pulls out a cell phone, texting.*]

ELI [CONT'D]

We need to develop a multi tiered system where every legal citizen has access to reasonable basic medical care, but if anyone wants more extensive care they would have to pay for it through private sources. In the end, there needs to be complete transparency in a field where too many consumers are uneasy questioning the cost of their medical care.

Health care is the only thing consumers really don't know what the cost is. It's really the same issue as stemming illegal immigration.

You can't fix it by patching it after the fact, with a wall or more border police. You need to address it at the source. The cost of health care could be contained... if we focus on everyone's health... and not on the cost.

RUDD

And in the remaining few seconds we have what you just mentioned...immigration? Do you favor a wall?

CUT TO:
FTP CONTROL ROOM:

[*everyone is actually following the interview.*]

                    DIRECTOR
                Camera 2, slow zoom in.

CUT TO:
MONITOR OF CAMERA 2:

                      ELI
We as a nation cannot just disenfranchise 10, 12 whatever
million illegal immigrants. I prefer to view them...

CUT TO:

GREEN ROOM & MONITOR:

[*Ann leaving in a huff, Russ tagging
behind.*]

                      ANN
            What in the hell just happened?

[*multitasking, texting, talking,
walking.*]

                     RUSS
        I'm not sure... but it may be a game changer.

ELI [CONT'D]

... so it's like fixing water in your basement. You can't truly make it right by patching the foundation at the border... you've got to divert the flow at the source by managing the flow in a different direction with inter-government cooperation and infrastructure investments to create opportunities. I would get Donald Trump to negotiate a plan to spread the costs and responsibilities.

RUDD

Any final thoughts you'd like to share before we close?

ELI

Mike, we've talked about a lot of issues, which seem in today's political environment to be unsolvable. At the bottom of most every issue though, is really the issue of population.

The more people in this country and the world, it becomes inevitable... that we experience more conflict in dealing with each other, and our social and legal systems just aren't equipped to deal with this increased level of conflict.

Simply put, we need to manage conflicting interests better, both domestically and globally, if we truly want to solve the serious issues like bloated government, political privilege and terrorism. I don't have all the answers, hell, I don't even know all the questions. I just want to jump in and try to improve the system for reconciling two sides to a conflict so we can make some progress by changing the gridlock culture in Washington.

The simple guide is the $Q=R \geq E$ equation, identify all expectations and then mobilize resources, money, people and ideas to create a reality that meets or exceeds those expectations and then evaluate all perspectives with a 760° view.

RUDD

OK, then... Eli, thank you for coming in this morning and good luck to you... I'm sure we'll be seeing more of you in the coming weeks and months and I'm sure the people of Fredericksburg thank you for your alertness.

ELI

Thanks for having me, Mike. ... and guys... *[pointing to the people behind the cameras, including Emily.]* let's go out for a beer later. I'd like to hear what you think.

RUDD

My apologies to Governor Ann Barrett for running over and I'm sure we'll be able to have the Governor on in the very near future to discuss gun control... or... should I say... managing the Second Amendment... and other important issues of the day... because it's Sunday, and time to... Face the Press.

DIRECTOR [Off screen]
We're off.

RUDD

[shaking his head and shaking Eli's hand.]

Fascinating stuff. I hope you're ready... I think things are going to get rather intense for you shortly.

[assistants taking mic off Rudd and hovering.]

RUDD [CONT'D]
Good luck to you.

[Eli is being ushered off set the back to green room, passes by Emily, again brushing up against each other, this time somewhat intentionally and both hold a glance for each other just a fraction of a second longer than being casual, Emily doesn't say anything directly to him, but clearly smitten, while Eli is still off in space after the FTP experience.]

ANN
Where did this guy come from?

RUSS
Not sure, but I'm gonna find out and take care of it.

CUT TO:

INTERIOR OF TV STUDIOS:

[Eli is being escorted out of the Face the Press Interview.]

[Ann is seen leaving TV studio in a huff, muttering to Russ and he is flustered.]

CUT TO:

ELI'S COMPUTER SCREEN:

[hundreds of e-mails are flooding into his inbox with requests for him to speak, visit, discuss, interviews, etc. all over the country.]

OUTSIDE IN NYC:

[*Eli is seen walking up 6th Ave and a professional political type approaches.*]

A.J.
Are you Eli Eaton?

ELI
Yes.

A.J.
I'm A.J. Bloom. I'm a political strategist. Can I buy you a cup of coffee?

ELI
I'm heading over to 57th for a bite at the Burger Joint.

A.J.
Mind if I tag along?

ELI
It's a free country... except on April 15th!

CUT TO:
INTERIOR OF BURGER JOINT:

[*very small hole in the wall dive.*]
[*sitting eating a burger... A.J. tries to pay, but Eli politely declines and pays for his own meal.*]

ELI
Sorry, I can't accept any freebies.

A.J.
You're becoming quite the sensation.

ELI
It's all quite surreal. This past August I was running my restaurant in Massachusetts... living a normal middle class life... and now... a couple months later... wow!

A.J.
Wow is right. Do you know what you need... now?

ELI
Sounds like you're about to tell me.

A.J.
You need guidance... direction... planning... a campaign committee... fund raising... the whole shebang... you need me to be your campaign director.

ELI
I'm always a little leery, when someone tells me... what... I... need.

A.J.

I don't think you realize what you're getting into... this isn't a high school election for student council. I've run two Senate campaigns, five Congressional and 3 Gubernatorial campaigns... and won seven of them. I've been following you on the social media and I believe you've got a good brand to exploit, but you're rough around the edges, a diamond in the rough, so to speak. It's crunch time. And time is ticking.

ELI

Any other worn out metaphors?

A.J.

Don't dismiss me, here. Elections are won on common metaphors and stuff people recognize. "There are things known and there are things unknown, and in between are the doors of perception." That's how you connect.

ELI

Thanks. Not interested. You're offering me the old, the tired, the worn out... it's not going to work much longer. But... thanks anyway for the Aldous Huxley quote. I prefer to paraphrase Frank... I'll do it my way.

A.J.

You have no idea how much you have to lose. There are a lot of sharks out there... and they're hungry and can smell blood a mile away. Trust me.

ELI

That's where you're wrong. I have absolutely nothing to lose... that's precisely why I may actually pull this off.

A.J.

You can't win if you're not legally registered with each state for the general election ballot.

ELI

That's the beauty of my plan... I don't have to qualify for any state ballots, I don't need a staff, I don't need any contributors, I don't want any contributions, I don't need an organization... or a manager.   All I need to do is use public pressure to convince the Presidential nominees to pick me as Vice President.

A.J.

I get that, but stuff comes up... you have no idea... you'll need help. Here's my card... think about it.

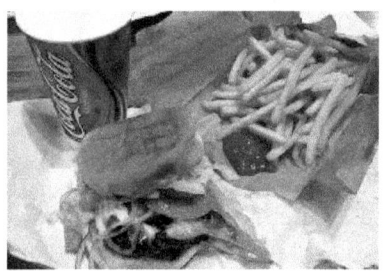

[*A.J. leaves, Eli leaves shortly thereafter, dumping his card in the trash bin along with the wrappings.*]

CUT TO:

HOTEL ROOM IN NYC:

[*Eli is packing, it's Monday AM and the taped FTP interview is playing in the background. Eli is having trouble watching himself on TV, talking on the phone with Matt.*]

ELI

Yeah... are you sure you recorded this? OK, I'll stop nagging. This is totally unreal. Yeah... I know. I'll be coming home later tonight... I'm really tired... need a break. It's been a long trip. Yeah... OK... I'll bring home a couple of those cookies. I'll see you later. Love ya.

CUT TO:

INTERIOR LEVAIN BAKERY:

MONDAY AM:

[*West Side Manhattan, Eli is purchasing a couple cookies for the trip home and he runs into Emily and her friend Beth on the way out. It's a cool morning outside and he decides to keep things going inside, with the lingering smell of cookies baking.*]

EMILY

Whoa... it's you.

ELI

Yeah... you, from yesterday.

EMILY

Hi... I'm Emily Morris... and this is my friend Beth. I see you are an aficionado of gourmet chocolate chip cookies... these are the absolute best.

ELI

I saw them on the Food Network last year and just had to try them... smells unbelievable in here. Oh, sorry, where are my manners... Hi, I'm Eli Eaton.

[*shakes her hand and Beth's.*]

[*in a playfully mocking tone.*]

EMILY

Yeah... you're from Pennsylvania and Massachusetts... and you're running for Vice President.

[*playfully in a similar to*ne.]

ELI
Oh... you've heard!

EMILY

Uh huh. And by the way... Governor Barrett is **REALLY** pissed at you.

ELI

I never said a word to her... oh.. check that... I did, but she totally ignored me... I don't think I was rude or anything. Besides, she owes me twenty bucks.

EMILY

It's not what you said... well... it's not what you may have said to her... it's what came out in the interview.

[*a bit sarcastically.*]
ELI

 What? She disagrees with one of my beliefs? No shock there.

EMILY

Well, it's more like... you stepped on her toes.

ELI

Huh? I do suck at dancing, but we never did the tango or anything. Did I say something she wanted to say? Oh... she's pissed because she got bumped and never got to say... anything, did she?

EMILY

Oh yeah... she's also pissed at you about that, too.

ELI

Too?

EMILY

Do you know why she was on the show?

ELI

Second Amendment?

EMILY

Oh... are you naive.. or what.

ELI

What?

EMILY

She's trying to run for President... and come in second... so she can be picked to be Vice President by the Republican nominee... kind of the anti-Laurie Plimpton and neutralize the women's vote as the VP nominee. She doesn't really think she has the delegates to win the nomination.

[Beth sees there is something going on and breaks off to purchase a cookie and in a tone almost like an ignored friend.]

BETH

Do you want a cookie while they're still warm... or are you two looking for something hotter... like sex?

[both Eli and Emily shoot her a look and then look at each other, blushing, as there is obviously something going on here.]

ELI

And what exactly are you to the Governor? You on her staff?

EMILY

Nah... not really. I'm doing a documentary on her... leading up to the 2016 Republican Convention.

ELI

So... you're in sync with her agenda?

EMILY

Oh... geeez no... it's just a job... she's playing way out in right field. I'm just in this for the rent money.

ELI
And you're playing... where?

EMILY
Left field. Standing more like... ooh, all the way near the left field line, in fact, maybe in the left field seats.

ELI
Got it. Kind of a James Carville Mary Matilan being married kind of thing goin on?

EMILY
Eyew no...nothing like that.

ELI
I mean political opposites.

EMILY
Oh.. yeah. Definitely opposites.

[*handing a bag to Emily, coy smile to Eli.*]

[*looking and smelling cookies in the bag, lamenting.*]

BETH
I hate to break up this foreplay, but we've got to get over to the Y so we can work off these cookies... which we haven't even eaten yet.

EMILY
Here's my card. I've got some footage of you at the interview yesterday... just in case you might want to use it sometime.... just don't say anything to the Governor... or Russ... it's kind of their dime, if you know what I mean.

ELI
Sure... I will.   I mean I won't. Thanks.

EMILY
Happy trails.

[*Emily and Beth exit the shop, she briefly almost involuntarily winks with both eyes at Eli, and as she walks away, does the quick look back... Eli stays momentarily as he doesn't want to appear to be following, looks intently at the card and puts it inside his wallet, nods like something good just happened and then leaves the shop.*]

21. Coming Full Circle

INTERIOR:
CAFETERIA AT WESTERN NEW ENGLAND UNIVERSITY, SPRINGFIELD, MA.

[Eli is visiting his son at college, now that he's been on national TV, the local media is following him and is taping while he is getting food and sitting down, groups of students come by and congratulate Eli, students taking notes, pictures, videos uploading to Instagram, Facebook, You Tube, Twitter, etc. One male, older than anyone in the crowd is texting, taking notes, pictures, while he lights up a cigarette, stays in background... kind of a shady looking character. Discussion is not about the issues, but about how Eli is now famous, kind of local boy makes it. Local TV crews are interviewing Eli, students are trying to get selfies with Eli and be on local TV news later, posturing in front of them.]

[wearing a "We're Eaton for VeeP" button.]

STUDENT REPORTER
Mr. Eaton, let me ask you, why do you think you can actually make a difference in Washington, when most everyone thinks it's hopeless.

ELI

Well, first, you have to understand the root cause of the current conflict between the Freedom Caucus on the Right and the Progressives like Bernie Sanders on the Left.

STUDENT REPORTER
... and that would be?

ELI

Back during the FDR era, society made a deal with itself, that in order to mitigate the severe economic impact of the Great Depression, we allowed government to step in and implement various forms of Socialism as a means to protect us, like Social Security. Once you open Pandora's box, well there's no way to close it and every year that passes a little more is added and over the years and the decades, government and social systems keep growing and growing, like any bureaucracy.

You wouldn't have to be Nostradamus back in the 1940's to project out that by 2016, some 75 years later, that big government and entitlements would grow way out of proportion... people always want more than before, not less. Now, the Right wants to draw a line in the sand and say, 'Hey, enough is enough, already', and the Left feels compassion for those in need and just can't say no. Think of government like your parents. You always want more from them, not less, so the real issue here is similar to parenting. Give you children everything you can at the risk of spoiling them, or be a hard ass and make them work for what they get and they hate you, but hope they grow up stronger and more self reliant. Personally, I see a valid position that needs addressed on both sides.

STUDENT REPORTER
OK, so how can any one person change things.

ELI

It's a simple equation... $Q=R\geq E$... First you ask questions to establish what their expectations are, then mobilize whatever resources in money, people and ideas are available to meet those expectations, and if you can't, then you need to show them how the other side isn't doing any better. It's a lot like parenting, you've got to treat each child equally while getting each one believing that they are getting the same... or more than the others. As long as both sides see that I'm truly independent and not aligned with the other side, it should work.

STUDENT REPORTER

Mr. Eaton, will you do a follow up interview for the campus radio station?

ELI

Sure, just let me grab a salad.

STUDENT REPORTER

Hey, is that older guy over there in the hat with you? He's definitely not faculty or staff here... and he's smoking.

ELI

Now that you mention it... no.

STUDENT REPORTER
I better have campus security check it out.

CUT TO:
INTERIOR COURTHOUSE OFFICE:

[*first person view, with only hands shown, holding folders and records at Hall of Justice courthouse... looking through a tall stack of folders, papers. Certain papers being photocopied, quarters being put into machine... copies stuffed in a new folder, EATON v. EATON written on tab, text message when folder is closed and placed in a briefcase, cell phone pulled out. and texting dialog*:]

SENDER CELL PHONE
Got him

RECEIVER CELL PHONE
U sure?

SENDER CELL PHONE
As you always say, break out the butter...He's toast!

CUT TO:
VIDEO:

[montage, Eli quick shots in every state, here ME, NH, VT, RI, MA and showing Interstate numbers and Welcome to... state signs.]

CUT TO:

INTERIOR:
PEPE'S APIZZA IN NEW HAVEN, CT:

[*Eli is sitting in a booth getting back to his 'roots' talking more one on one, but everyone is stopping by for a selfie, a handshake... he is definitely a public figure now. On the table is a tomato pie and a white clam pie.*]

PATRON
I don't agree with everything you're talking about... but you seem to be a straight shooter... honest.

ELI
Thanks... I couldn't ask for any more. Just say exactly that to any pollsters, family and friends... and as we get closer to the conventions, and there isn't anyone else you'd rather support, I'd appreciate yours... and **be sure to ask any of the Presidential candidates to take the pledge for selecting an independent bi-partisan Vice President!**

PATRON
Sounds like a plan... Good luck to you. We gotta a couple extra slices, want them?

ELI
Thanks, but I've got a tomato pie to go. Be well.

[Eli goes to the counter to pick up a take-out pizza. The manager as he hands the box to Eli.]

MANAGER
This is on the house... I like what you're doing.

ELI
Thanks, that's very nice of you, but I can't accept any freebies, no matter how thoughtful. If I accept free food, then you and others would expect that I'd accept other stuff from special interests... and I don't want to owe anything to anyone. My whole campaign needs to be totally transparent and independent. No scandals. That's why I'm doing it alone and don't even accept any campaign contributions.

MANAGER
Gotta give you credit... you are different!

ELI
Hope you mean that in a good way!

MANAGER
Sure do... Good luck to you... I'll be voting for you.

ELI
Thanks... just tell all your customers and friends and ask any Presidential candidates that might come in, **Will you support picking an independent bi-partisan Vice President if you get the nomination?**

CUT TO:

[Eli is checking his cell phone, looking at a new text message just that arrived, then contorts his face, not comprehending the meaning of a text message from an anonymous source, then shakes it off.]

ELI'S CELL PHONE
EE... U R B ing investigated

[Eli takes his change and exits the restaurant, taking another look at the just received text message, slowly putting the phone in his pocket, looking puzzled.]

CUT TO:

EXTERIOR:
PARKING LOT AT COSTCO:

[Eli is going to shake hands, etc. for coming and going customers, walking around sampling the free samples, talking...]

[*shaking hands with customers coming and going.*]

ELI

Hi... I'm Eli Eaton... I'm from Pennsylvania and Massachusetts and I'm running for Vice President. What's the most important thing on your mind about the federal government?

22. Reality TV

[*Montage of TV shows: OReilly, Dennis Miller, Anderson Cooper, Ellen, Maddow, John Oliver, Steven Colbert, Trevor Noah, Larry Wilmore, Seth Myers, Jimmy Kimmel, Jimmy Fallon etc.*]

CUT TO:
INTERIOR: **SET OF TV SHOW**

HOST
... and good luck to you... Eli Eaton everyone!

CUT TO:
HALLWAY OF TV STUDIO:

[*Eli bumps into Ann, Russ, Emily and Dave.*]

ANN
Mr. Eaton... just saw the show... you're really making some waves out there.

[*a bit surprised she actually knows and acknowledges him now.*]

ELI
Guess so, I just hope I don't get sea sick.

[*Emily and Eli lock eyes for just a moment.*]

ANN

I just wanted to thank you... I understand you were the one who reported those terrorists on July 4th. I was there and I... well, just wanted to thank you for saving lives there, mine included.

[*Emily is also thanking him, but with her eyes and body language.*]

ELI

I only did what any responsible adult should have done, to be honest, it was a tough call, but as it turned out, the right one.

RUSS

Mr. Eaton, I've just received an offer from the show "Some Time with Bob Mayor" to have you and the Governor to do a special event show, a high energy point counter point kind of thing, where the two of you can mix it up and Mayor will moderate... and probably take shots at both of you... but hey, there is no such thing as bad publicity, is there? What do you think?... I know you don't have a manager... I think it would be good for both of you... the Governor's delegate numbers are steadily climbing and you're not doing too shabby anymore, either.

ELI

You'd better keep an eye on that left hand.

[*Emily smirks a bit, getting the left handed compliment joke and gives Eli a fond glance, which he realizes that she is the only one who got it... although Ann also got it, and now Ann is seeing Eli in more favorable personal light and someone she can use later.*]

[*moving her hands like wrestling back and forth.*]

ANN

Eli... I'll keep Russ in line... I think it would be fun... you and me... mixing it up.

[*with a quick glance past her to Emily.*]

ELI
OK, I'm in.

RUSS
Great... I'll take care of the details, I'll be in touch... It'll happen sooner than later, Mayor is hot on this.

ELI
Just give me a couple days notice.

[*as they go their separate ways, Emily and Eli brush by one another, it's now their thing to connect, Emily blinking again involuntarily and holding the glance a second longer... and the quick look back, just like at the bakery.*]

[*video montage of visiting states:
showing notable sites in NY, NJ, DE &
MD.*]

CUT TO:
SET OF SOME TIME WITH BOB MAYOR:

[*Eli and Ann are sitting at an oval table together with Mayor
off to the side. Good chemistry developing, both politically
and otherwise. Curious sparks developing between Ann and
Eli... Emily is not pleased.*]

[*Mayor showing video montage of visiting states showing
notable sites in NC, SC, GA, FL, AL, MS,, TN, LA, AR, TX
calendar passing from 2015 later in year into 2016.*]

[*video montage of visiting states showing notable sites in OK,
MO, IA, IL, WI, MI, MN, calendar passing into Spring 2016.*]

INT: **LIVE STUDIO SET:**

[*Bob Mayor is moderating, Ann and Eli are really getting
into it, with Bob injecting his brand of humor, being seen on
a TV monitor, no dialog but Ann and Eli are yucking it up but
nothing can be actually heard until...*]

CUT TO:
FOCUS ON MAYOR:

MAYOR
Well... We've been having a great time tonight bull shitting
our way though all the major issues facing our country, but
for the last part of the show, I'd like to get serious for a
moment...

AUDIENCE
Boooo.

MAYOR
OK, OK... just for a moment, then we'll get back to our two polar opposites... actually they've been more like two polar bears... in heat... wow... have you seen the sparks flying tonight? ... reminds me of the Northern Lights... on Viagra!

AUDIENCE
Cheers and whooping it up.

MAYOR
So tell me you two kids... Eli, we know what your intentions are... but Governor... are you running for President, or are you really positioning yourself for Vice President to counter the Laurie Plimpton effect?

[*leaning over toward her in a rather obvious seductive Groucho Marx way trying to get her to divulge a secret, winking at the audience.*]

MAYOR (CONT'D)
You can tell me, I won't tell anyone.

AUDIENCE
Cheers and whoops it up.

ANN
Bob, if you're trying to seduce me... into divulging my intentions, you're going to at least have to buy me dinner first! [*Winks at Bob.*]

AUDIENCE
Woohooo. [*Whooping it up.*]

MAYOR
Well, if that's all it's going to take, I've got a meal replacement bar back in my dressing room!

AUDIENCE
Woo Woo Woo Woo.

ANN
Well, Bob.. if that's all the game you've got... then you're going to have to wait for the wedding night.

AUDIENCE
More whooping it up.

MAYOR
Already been there, done that. Costs too much in alimony!

AUDIENCE
Cheering, applauding.

ANN
Bob, you've got to pay for it... one way or another.

MAYOR
... and on that note, I want to thank Eli Eaton... who is running for... well... everything... no... he's running for Vice President.. and he's willing to swing both ways... [*applause.*] and Governor Ann Barrett, who is just looking sexy and is running for.... well, just running in the upcoming Marathon, but don't worry, she won't finish til after the 5 hour mark.

AUDIENCE
Oooooh.... Too soon, still too soon.

MAYOR
OK...OK... Sorry Boston...
Thank you all, you've been great and good night everyone!

[*upbeat Some Time with Bob Mayor
theme starts plays as people start to
exit.*]

AUDIENCE
Rising, standing O, applauding, cheering.
CUT TO:

[*Emily and Dave are packing up the
equipment, Eli is walking away from
the set, Emily moves to intercept him
but Ann comes up to him first.*]

ANN
That was good... a lot of good energy out there...I'm sorry to
see it end.

ELI
I agree...Bob was right... lot of sparks out there.

ANN
You felt sparks?

ELI
Oh yeah, I don't think we see eye to eye on everything, but
that's good... makes things really intense, interesting, kinda
like James Carville and Mary Matalin.

ANN
Would you be interested in going out for a late snack and a
drink?

ELI
Sure, I am a bit parched after that. There's a bar at the hotel... meet you there in say... 30 minutes?

ANN
Perfect.

CUT TO:

23. The Dessert Club

HOTEL BAR AREA:

[inside a small cozy dimly lit pub area, Eli and Ann are sitting at a small table, she's drinking a white wine spritzer, Eli is having a beer and they touch glasses.]

ANN
Here's to uncommitted delegates and high poll numbers.

ELI
So... I'm a bit surprised you wanted to see each other off camera. Rumor has it you were really pissed off at me at Face the Press.

ANN
Oh, that... ancient history... I was really pissed off at Rudd more than anything, but now... it's actually worked out to my advantage.

ELI
How's that?

ANN
My delegate numbers are rising... polls are stronger and now he's really kissing my ass to get me back on. There's a real chance now I could get the nomination if things fall into place... Changes everything!

ELI
Amazing how often bad things seem to always work out for the best.

[*Eli fumbles a little bit realizing the faux pas, given her husband was murdered a couple years ago or so, she recognizes it, and knowingly waves him off and Eli is starting to believe he may actually be on the right path. The nonverbal exchange makes for a more intimate conversation.*]

ANN
I must say, I'm getting more and more impressed with you, every time I see you.

ELI
Thanks.

ANN
Nice delivery, nice rapport with the audience, honest eyes... nice butt.

ELI
Mrs. Robinson, are you trying to seduce me?!?

ANN
Seduction is not in my vocabulary these days. I can't believe how hard it is to get laid after your husband is murdered... and then... when you're running for the White House... [*pointing to the Secret Service agent over there*.] the old male double standard... I hate it.

ELI
Oh... something tells me you could figure out a policy strategy here.

ANN
I'd laugh if I wasn't so horny.

[*she finishes her drink and the server*
brings her another one and removes
the empty glasses.]

ANN [CONT'D]
Listen, have you ever experienced the erotic pleasure of
giving a woman a good foot massage?

ELI

Yeah... and If you think my delivery is good, you should
check out my hands.

ANN
Oh, you have so much to learn, grasshopper. I'm not talking
about your hands. Are you a member of the Dessert Club?

[*suddenly realizes he is missing*
something.]

ELI
We're not talking about key lime pie here, are we?

ANN
Think of it like the dinner version... of the Mile High Club.

ELI
Oh.

[*she moves just a bit closer to Eli and whispers eye to eye*
while we see her kick off one of her shoes and extend her leg
under the table toward Eli... then we see Eli's face and all of
the sudden his eyes open widely... when her leg makes
contact... he then realizes the foot massage doesn't involve
the hands at all... he starts breathing heavy, getting glassy
eyed, then a pause in the action...]

ANN

I can't tell you how much I want you to touch me right now.

[*Eli inches even closer and briefly brushes his nose on her cheek and then we see Ann take hold of Eli's foot under the table, takes his shoe off and slowly moves his foot to her and her eyes slowly close when contact is made under the table... we see both now resume their heavy breathing, she purses her lips as both whisper somewhat restrained oohs and aahs while they hold hands, until...*]

ANN [CONT'D]

whew... and before you ask, and I know you will... I'm wearing pink... wet pink, very wet pink.

SLOW FADE OUT:
THEN FADE IN TO:

INTERIOR OF BREAKFAST AREA OF HOTEL:

[*next AM, in the breakfast dining room of the hotel, Eli is sitting eating scrambled eggs and a waffle by himself, Emily comes quickly right up to his table, virtually standing over him, pausing, waiting for recognition...*]

EMILY
How could you?

ELI
How could I what? Oh... and good morning to you, too.

EMILY

How could you.. go off with... with... [*after choosing her words carefully and now lowering her tone*]   what she said last night?

ELI

She said a lot of things... anything in particular?

[*pausing, glancing away as what she's saying is not what she means in a lower tone.*]

EMILY

The second class citizen thing.

ELI

Would you be referring to the discussion on immigration reform?

EMILY

Don't try to be charming with me, you know what I mean.

ELI

Sit... Please... We can discuss... You look hot... under the collar... that is, and I'd hate to see you jump into a good debate on an empty stomach. I don't have any New York chocolate chip cookies, but I could get you a yogurt with granola.

EMILY

That would be great... but that's not the point.

[she sits, *Eli motions the server over to the table.*]

ELI

I noticed you had some vanilla yogurt with chocolate chip granola on the menu... could you please bring us one.

SERVER

Certainly. I'll be right back. Anything to drink, Ma'am?

EMILY

Just some organic orange juice, please.

ELI

Now... you can't be this upset over immigration, so what's really bugging you?

EMILY

I thought you were different. I thought you really cared about... people... had more compassion.

ELI

... and now you think I don't... because of...

[*she starts personally upset, then she relaxes and continues...*]

EMILY

How can you... agree to have second class citizenship for the illegal immigrants?

ELI

May I ask you a question?

EMILY

I know what you're doing... you do this every time you try to convince someone of something. Ask questions, figure out their expectations and then hit 'em with an idea that matches their expectations.

ELI
Am I that transparent?

EMILY
... but it works... and I don't want it to work on me. Go ahead and ask. I feel like a newbie playing chess against a grand master... and I'm going to resign my position in about four or five moves... and the answer to your question is... maybe... will be... obviously, yes.

ELI
I haven't even asked it, yet.

EMILY
It doesn't matter... you know the answer is going to be yes.

[*with a slight nod and wink.*]

ELI
I'm gonna remember that for future reference!

[*pause*]

ELI [CONT'D]
Do you have these conversations with yourself often?

[*Emily pauses briefly, realizing it's
nice to share with someone else who is
intelligent and that she's been rather
isolated for too long.*]

EMILY
I'm a good conversationalist... once I get going.

ELI

I can see that. It's nice to be able to go back and forth... with someone else, though.

[*Emily is thinking... OMG he got me.*
She feels exposed and vulnerable, now
the truth is finally coming out.]

EMILY
How could you?

ELI
Here we go again. Have we done a 360... or are we going off on what you really want to talk about?

[*Eli knows what she is getting at, but*
not letting her off the hook, just yet.]

[*she is finally breaking down for an*
honest conversation.]

EMILY
Do you really think I'm hot... under the collar, that is?

ELI
Oh yeah... I felt something the first time we met when we brushed up against each other at the Face the Press studio... it was nice. You were wearing the dark tan cargo shorts, not too tight but showed off your nice legs and the sleeveless green top looked like you go to the Y.
I think you winked at me... actually, it was probably more of a blink, I smiled back, but anyway, yeah... I think you're hot... period, and forget the collar part.

EMILY
Then how could you go out with that tea party nut case last night?

ELI

You're so cute... when you're jealous... it's becoming.

EMILY

I'm serious... thanks.

ELI

Listen, Annie...

EMILY

Annie... now you're calling her Annie?

[*Eli takes her hand and holds it
calmly. The server comes with the
food, and to the server.*]

ELI

Thank you.

SERVER

Anything else?

ELI

No... I think...finally we're good here.

[*impatiently.*]

EMILY

Not yet, we aren't. Annie?

ELI

... and I'm going to assume you're not looking for a review of
the Broadway musical here... as I was saying, Ann... the
Governor... OK? is the cheerleader and the most popular girl
in high school that every boy in the school wants to nail... but
you know that only the football team gets to screw her.

[*thinking back to the first comment
made by the Gov. at Face the Press.*]

EMILY
I knew it.

ELI
Knew what?

EMILY
Never mind... go on.

ELI
I just find it humorously ironic that now... all the guys on the football team are fat, bald and selling life insurance... and after all these years, the geeks are rich, fit and finally get a chance.

EMILY
You consider yourself a geek?

ELI
Definitely... and proud of it.

EMILY
So now you have a chance to nail the blond prom queen?

ELI
Well, if last night is any indication... yeah, I guess so.

EMILY
So... did you?

[*Eli shoots her a long stare.*]

EMILY [CONT'D]
I'm sorry, that was rude.

ELI
I had to go out with her last night. Let's face it... she now has a shot at getting the nomination and I need to keep things... shall we say... open with her.

[*under her breath, in a snarky tone.*]

EMILY
Yeah, like her legs.

[*Eli just now realizes he has been holding her hand, just a little too long and slowly backs off, but she moves to pull it back.*]

ELI
Listen, my whole candidacy depends on my being 100% independent and I can't risk anything that would tie me to either party until the conventions are over. Sadly, that includes her staff, even if that someone... isn't even aligned politically with her. I can't afford to get caught up with any scandals of any kind... not even a whisper wrapped in a hint of a rumor.

EMILY
I really hate politics right now.

ELI
Right now... I do too... you have no idea.

[*somewhat sheepishly.*]

EMILY

You really think I'm hot?

CUT TO:
[*view of cell phone screen in a male's
hand, texting with thumbs.*]

SENDER CELL PHONE

When r we gonna spring this info?
                        Time not ripe, yet.
R getting antsy.
                    Hold on... not til he peaks.
                    It's all in the timing.
He's getting nervous.
                    Control him.
OK

CUT TO:

[*video montage of visiting states showing notable sites in KS,
NE, SD, ND, MT, ID, WY.*]

24. Your Past is Your Future

RESTAURANT:

[*sometime in the later primary season of 2016 just before the conventions. Eli is holding one his typical meetings, part personal part public, they usually end with an informal press conference, as both the print media and TV and social media bloggers are following his every move now.*]

ELI
Does anyone have any questions, you'd like to put on the table?

[*asked in the same mode as Eli does to establish the expectation of the person.*]

REPORTER
Yes, may I ask a question?

ELI
Go for it.

[*nudging cameraman to focus in... for the kill.*]

REPORTER
Do you feel the morality of our public office holders is a material basis for choosing our elected representatives?

ELI
I certainly do.

REPORTER

OK... then, does a politician have the moral and ethical responsibility to divulge everything about their past so that we can judge how they would lead us in the future?

ELI

Well, within reason... I'm sure we all have made some questionable decisions in our youths... but to answer your question, I think the public does have a right to know what we have done as adults, what we've learned from our mistakes, our successes and take responsibility for our behavior.

REPORTER

As a member of the press... I couldn't agree more.

ELI

See... we can reach consensus in this country.

[*crowd cheers loudly.*]

REPORTER

... and you still are a strong supporter of women's rights and equal opportunity and getting along instead of bickering, fighting and taking advantage of others?

ELI

Roger to all of those... yes... absolutely.

[*now in an accusatorial tone.*]

REPORTER

So... Mr. Eaton, how do you respond to a story that has just come out, that fifteen years ago, when you were an adult, in your thirties, there was a personal restraining order taken out against you, to prevent further physical injury against a woman?

[*an instant gasp and huge hush comes over the crowd.*]

[a *bit taken back, but after a moment he gathers himself.*]

ELI

That part of my life involves a custody thing with my son and another child... and for their protection I'd rather not get into that. My son does not deserve to be drawn into that controversy. My son is not running for office, I am. I would ask that you respect his privacy and leave all that be. *[somewhat shaken.]* Thank you everyone, I'm going try one of the shrimp tacos... They look and smell fantastic.

[*crowd is still supportive , but clearly not to the previous level by about 50% than before the question, while Eli exits promptly, obviously shaken.*]

CUT TO:

LOCAL RESTAURANT:

[two days later at the end of another town meeting at a local restaurant.]

ELI
Thank you everyone... thank you very much for your interest and your support. I'm going to try some of the BBQ... smells great.

AUDIENCE
One last question, Mr. Eaton.

ELI
Sure.

AUDIENCE
How do you respond to a second report from this afternoon, that about 15 years ago, a second restraining order was taken out by a child to prevent physical abuse and sexual molestation?

ELI
As I said the other day, this involved minor children at the time and has no bearing on my running for Vice President. The emotional welfare of the children involved should be respected and kept out of any public discussion.

AUDIENCE 2
That's the second one, isn't it?

ELI
Same issue... please respect their privacy. I won't comment on any of that.

CUT TO:

[*view of e-mail from A.J. saying, "I told you. Please give me a call."*]

[*local TV covering Eli's activities the following day.*]

REPORTER
...and campaigning in our area today, was Eli Eaton, who is running for Vice President for both parties' nomination and is still gathering quite a crowd out at the Hillside Mall food court... yet now possibly reminiscent of Herman Cain, who after shooting up in the polls to lead the pack during the 2012 campaign, was forced to withdraw in the wake of nagging personal issues, now, a third report of a personal restraining order from Eli Eaton's past has surfaced this morning... this one taken out on behalf of his own son, to prevent physical abuse and sexual molestation... of his own child. People are now talking about the Cosby effect, it's getting so bad.

CUT TO:

[*cell phone screen, person watching news- cast in background.*]

CELL PHONE SCREEN
What time is it, kids???

??????

It's Jerry Sandusky time
the bastard's going down

good job

they even picked up on the Cosby ref
fabulous

i feel like a Godfather's pizza!

CUT TO:

[*montage of headlines, blogs, TV commentary on the three restraining orders, comment by late night hosts re: rise and fall of Eli Eaton, question his candidacy, demand for answers or to withdraw from race in disgrace... a lot of piling on clips of Eli avoiding question, making him look guilty... included is dark shot of computer screen.*]

COMPUTER SCREEN
did we miss boat on this 1 letting him go viral?
dnk
pull plug?
wait day or 2
same o same o politicians
may b

CUT TO:

CAMPAIGN OFFICE WATCHING NEWS CHANNEL ON TV:

TV PUNDIT 1
A little later this afternoon, Eli Eaton, who has been running for Vice President as an independent seeking the nomination for **BOTH** parties... is having a press conference. Mr. Eaton has been under significant scrutiny by the same media who turned him into an overnight sensation, for alleged physical abuse against three different people 15 years ago, the latest involving his own son.

TV PUNDIT 2

He's going to withdraw... he has no choice. The media is quick to build you up, and it's equally brutal and will also take you down in a heartbeat. How much have you heard from Cosby, lately?

TV PUNDIT 3

I don't see any other option, either. I've seen copies of these three different restraining orders and unless they've been photo shopped or faked somehow, and I doubt that's the case, he has to withdraw...

TV PUNDIT 2

He hasn't denied them... they must be real... maybe someone else will try his radical approach to winning the Vice Presidency, but it certainly looks like Eli Eaton's journey is about to end.

TV PUNDIT 3

I agree Eli will be gone later today, but I must say, his vision of a productive independent Vice President may live for another day, even if the visionary walks off into the sunset.

TV PUNDIT 1

Stay tuned, we will carry the press conference live at 4PM... and we'll be back after these messages.

CUT TO:

INTERIOR HOTEL BALLROOM:

[*press conference with a overflow audience, huge bundle of microphones at the podium, Eli walks up to podium, somber demeanor. Flashes are taken as...*]

CUT TO:

BARRETT CAMPAIGN OFFICE:

[*she is watching TV, Emily and Dave are shooting her watching the press conference: Both Emily and Ann are somber.*]

CUT TO:

25. Truth and Consequences

VIDEO CLIPS:

[*Matt's campus center, large group watching TV, and quick montage of places we've seen before, restaurants where he first got started, familiar people concerned with what is about to come, some tears flowing, as though life flashing before his eyes just before dying. Cut back to Barrett's campaign office, viewing TV as Eli begins...*]

ON TV MONITOR:

ELI

First, I'd like to thank everyone for coming this afternoon. I believe it is a testament to our country, our nation and our political process that a complete picture can be provided to the public about all of our candidates seeking public office... so let me cut right to the chase. Recently, there have been three allegations of abuse that have been brought to the public's attention regarding personal restraining orders against me by three different persons, two of whom were minors at the time.

I think it's a shame that matters involving children, that are supposed to be sealed from the public for their protection, can be illegally secured and disseminated to the public for the purely personal political gain of some back room politician who is trying to protect his own interests, all contrary the public good. It's a shame... and only the children suffer from all this.

So shame... shame... shame on whomever felt it necessary to violate the personal welfare of children who have done nothing to deserve any of this media focus. But let me address these allegations, directly and forthrightly, just as you would want from your public officials.

[*long pause as he takes a deep breath and exhales.*]

Each and every one of the three restraining orders that have been circulating in the media about me from 15 years ago [*another pause.*] are sadly, neither faked nor photo shopped... they're all quite real.

[*large gasp, cameras start snapping, flashing, oohs, aahs drawn out.*]

CUT TO:

[*darkened room in a campaign office.*]

STAFFFER
Got that cocksucker!

CUT TO:

BARRETT'S CAMPAIGN OFFICE TV:

[*Emily appears heartbroken, Ann is grimacing.*]

ELI [CONT'D]

But... no matter the consequences, you deserve the whole story. You... *[opening his arms to encompass everyone.]* the public, deserve the truth... the whole truth, and nothing but the truth, **SO HELP ME GOD.**

Although the existence of those restraining orders is real, each and every allegation made, in each and every one of those three restraining orders is totally, 100% false. Period, no exceptions. The false allegations were made by someone who had serious issues before the family court and felt it was necessary to lie... and make up false allegations and fraudulent injuries in order to gain an unfair advantage in a very contentious custody case involving my son. She took advantage of and misused her role as a parent for her own agenda, both personal... and financial, along with an unscrupulous attorney to gain an unfair tactical advantage in that custody case, because sadly, in family court, any man accused is guilty until proven innocent, but that's a serious discussion we as a country have to have another place and time.

As a result of those falsified allegations, I was unable to see or even talk to my son for more than two years, while she attempted to alienate my son against me during that whole time. It took me five years... five effin years... to gather up the independent physical evidence to refute each and every one of the false allegations made against me, but I did... and I ultimately prevailed. And when I did, the judge, a woman I might add... awarded me... sole legal and sole physical custody of my son, it was so bad. That was over ten years ago.

I have here, with me, all the independent papers, court orders, judgments, pictures, videos and other evidence from the court, the court appointed investigators and the court appointed psychologist and guardians ad litem reports that prove beyond any shadow of a doubt whatsoever, that everything I am stating here this afternoon is the truth, the whole truth... and nothing but the truth, so help me God. 60 Minutes has asked me to do an in depth interview this Sunday to review all of this evidence and I have agreed to do that interview and invite everyone to watch that interview and make up your own minds.

Lastly, in case there is any shred of doubt on this issue, I challenge anyone involved with these restraining orders to come forward and we can have a public lie detector examination given to all of us... by the leading FBI polygraph examiner in the country, and that person can ask the same appropriate questions to all of us, in public for all to see and hear and judge. Total and absolute public transparency. That's how confident I am. I have already passed four different lie detector examinations during that period and I seriously doubt anyone will take me up on my offer at this time, but if they do, I am ready anywhere, anytime, anyplace. In closing, I have only one more thing to say...

[*brief pause*]

I'm Eli Eaton... I'm from Pennsylvania and Massachusetts... *[he pulls out a hot dog and holds it up.]* and I'm Eaton for Vice President of the United States of America!

[*Eli takes a demonstrative bite out of the hot dog, Significant groundswell of applause and cheering, cameras clicking, flashes and as Eli begins to leave the podium.*]

ELI [CONT'D]
...and if you'll excuse me, all of the sudden I feel like having a burrito bowl at Chipotle.

CUT TO:

26. Talking Heads

INTERIOR:
BARRETT CAMPAGIN OFFICE:

[*Emily wiping her eyes, Ann smiling, nodding, cut to dark room, staffer throws the cell phone across the room in disgust, computer screen shows...*]

CUT TO:
COMPUTER SCREEN:

COMPUTER SCREEN

take this viral
he's good people... my cuz went thru same thing
with his kid. done

CUT TO:
TV :

REPORTER 1
We have just been listening to Eli Eaton, who is running for Vice President responding to multiple allegations found in three separate personal abuse restraining orders.

REPORTER 2
Never saw that coming.

CUT TO:

EVENING NEWS:

ANCHOR

In a stunning turn of events earlier this afternoon, Vice Presidential candidate Eli Eaton, who was expected to withdraw from the race resulting from multiple allegations of physical abuse, came out swinging and quite possibly made his bid even more compelling. For the story we go to...

[*video montage of headlines, comments, late night tv quips, from Fallon, Kimmel and Colbert, etc.*]

CUT TO:
PLIMPTON CAMPAIGN OFFICE:

[*later that week, in a hotel room on the eve of the Democratic Convention, close in on TV monitor with TV news type program on, all activity stops while...*]

TV PUNDIT 1

As you have probably heard... earlier this morning, in yet another unexpected turn of events in a year where the unexpected has become the new norm... former real estate tycoon and New York first term Senator Mario Ruiz announced his withdrawal from the race for President and unconditionally released all of his committed delegates, a week before the Republican national convention, effectively guaranteeing the first Republican convention in forty years where the Republican nominee will be decided by a vote of delegates on the floor at the Republican Convention. A year and a half ago, we started with 15, and now we're down to the final two...Governor Jay Cashman and Governor Ann Barrett.

TV PUNDIT 2

If you're looking for drama, it doesn't get any better than this. On the eve of the Democratic Convention, you gotta give Senator Ruiz credit for bringing back the media attention to the Republicans... and believe me, they won't forget this in 2020 if Laurie wins in November.

Everyone thought that Senator Ruiz would be the dealmaker leading up to the convention, but now, in an unbelievably selfless act, designed to bring the full force of the media attention back to the Republican Convention, he is certainly setting up a future run. But now... the last time a contested vote was taken at a Republican Convention was way back in 1976, when dark horse Ronald Reagan almost won the nomination from incumbent President, Gerald Ford. Forty years is a long time, and there's an entire generation that hasn't witnessed the drama of a real convention battle... the Republicans couldn't have scripted this any better... and Sen. Ruiz... clearly the frontrunner for 2020... it is his nomination to lose after this.

TV PUNDIT 3

Just as the coronation of Laurie Plimpton is about to take place, all eyes are now re-focused in anticipation of the Republican Convention next week, where Sen. Ruiz's delegates are up for grabs, both Governor Cashman and Governor Barrett are going to have to scramble to get those delegates into their respective camps, effectively making the Democratic Convention second page news.

TV PUNDIT 1

That's right... about the only drama now for the Democrats is who will be Laurie Plimpton's choice for Vice President... will she be influenced by the overwhelming popular voter support for the recently vindicated Eli Eaton... or will she stick with tradition and fill the ticket for Vice President with a political ally of her own choice?

TV PUNDIT 2

Tradition? You know the speculation... what would happen if she chose her brother, former President Will Plimpton for Vice President... talk about breaking tradition. She's playing her cards close to the vest, though.

CUT TO:
PLIMPTON'S OFFICE:

STAFF 1
We should have anticipated this.

STAFF 2

We're going to have to create some of our own drama... it's crunch time, a decision has to be made.

STAFF 1
When is she getting here?

STAFF 3
I just got a text... she's on her way... be here in 30.

STAFF 1
OK then... we've got thirty minutes to figure out who is our best go for Vice President.

STAFF 2

It's the same three choices...hasn't changed... we've got Larry, Moe and Curly.

STAFF 1

Listen, Will brings the same voters...maybe some nostalgia votes but has all the baggage... and there's the legal issue of the 22nd Amendment.

STAFF 2

There's really no legal issue, if Will is VP, if necessary, he can legally assume the Presidency... he just can't be **ELECTED** President more than twice...

STAFF 1

Still, we're exposed... it's still going to look like FDR packing the Supreme Court...not good.

STAFF 2

Ernie Hernandez is the safe choice. He brings the Hispanic and African American vote, and he's controllable.

STAFF 1

Not as much an issue, now that Ruiz is out, we've probably got those votes now, anyway.

STAFF 2

... and the great wild card... Eli Eaton?

STAFF 1

Man, that could so go either way... either he's a visionary... or a pimple on my son's butt.

STAFF 3

The numbers don't lie... quite the contrary.

STAFF 1
Please...this guy is nothing more than a clown.

STAFF 2
She could just put him out to pasture.

STAFF 3
The bottom line is this guy has been making waves now for over a year, he's been totally vetted by Barrett's people... and he's come out of it even stronger... let's face it, he'll never be able to do anything he's talking about, but he brings a good cross party independent block of voters to the table... and what harm can he do. If he just shuts his pie hole and attends funerals.

STAFF 1
... and is only a heartbeat away from the Oval Office... really?

STAFF 3
This is gonna sound crazy... but...

CUT TO:

27. Mexican Standoff

PLIMPTON OFFICE:

[*later, Eli talking with Laurie's campaign team.*]

CAMPAIGN MANAGER [WAYNE]
Eli, because of your status, we've invited you in here to talk with Mrs. Plimpton... but first, there are some things **we** need to talk about.

ELI
OK, thanks.

WAYNE
So here's the drill. What's it going to take to get you to go away.

ELI
Excuse me?

WAYNE
Bottom line is the country can't afford to have you a heartbeat away from the Presidency. You just don't have the chops or the experience for the job.

STAFF 1
The Presidency, that is...but to be perfectly honest, you as Vice President... well... if Sarah Palin could've been Vice President... you get my drift, but the President of the United States? No way.

[*after an awkward moment where they
expect Eli to respond...*]

ELI
I'm just keeping an eye on your left hand.

STAFF 1
Nothing personal.

[*Eli bites his tongue, shaking his head
a bit.*]

ELI
[*sarcastically.*]　　　Yeah, right.

WAYNE
You're not as big as you'd like to think you are.

STAFF 1
Mr. Eaton...

ELI
Please, call me Eli... I'm not a formal kind of guy. I connect
with people on a personal level.

STAFF 1
OK, Eli... Listen, you're playing in the big league here, on
the national stage, not some local town council dealing with
zoning by-laws.

STAFF 2
Eli...the country has real issues and needs real players to get
the job done. Three hundred twenty million people in this
country rely on us to make their lives safe and meaningful.

STAFF 3
That doesn't even include the other six billion people on the
planet who depend on the United States to insure some
measure of security in their lives.

STAFF 1

So we have the final Jeopardy! question of the day. How does a small restaurant owner from Western Massachusetts fit into the big picture?

WAYNE

So, Mr. Eaton... Eli... What if we can arrange a position for you where you'll receive $1,000,000 in salary over the next four years. You won't have to do anything but deposit your money in the bank. You can re-open your restaurant and be set for life. All you have to do is announce that you're giving up on this Don Quixote quest, fade away and let the adults get down to business. Simple, neat and clean.

STAFF 1

Frankly, you're just a distraction in the larger scope of things.

[*after a long moment of reflection...*]
ELI

Gentlemen... and Laurie, Jay, if you're listening... and I'm sure you are...

[*surprised/embarrassed reactions
show Eli is onto something.*]

ELI [CONT'D]

You guys make a horrible good cop bad cop team... you really need to work on that... I'm not in this for the glory or the money. But trusting this whole dramatic thing you just came up with here is some kind of weird political Rorschach test... OK, not bad. So let's just cut to the chase...

CLOSE UP ON ELI:

ELI [CONT'D]

First... If both of you tap me to be the VP... and I am the only one who can pull that off this year... the race is simple math... Jay v. Laurie... no extraneous VP debates, no surprises, no Sarah Palins, no Thomas Eagletons, no embarrassing VP screw ups, no baggage, just Bush versus Clinton, Hatfield versus McCoy... mano a mano. Whoever gets the best of California, Florida, Wisconsin, Ohio, Colorado, Virginia and Pennsylvania gets the White House... The only smart thing for both of you is to have a neutral VP which can't hurt your respective campaigns.

I've got things I want to do... tax reform, immigration reform, health care reform and smoothing over the partisan gridlock mentality that has taken over the capital. Sure, I may get stonewalled, I may not be taken seriously up on the hill... I could end up like Jimmy Carter, but as God is my witness, I will not go down without a fight. Lady and gentleman, it's time to put on the gloves and get into the ring. So, Laurie... come in here and make the big decision. In case you haven't heard, I'm Eli Eaton, from Pennsylvania and Massachusetts and I'm still running for Vice President... and I hope I passed the audition.

WAYNE
... and the question of the Presidency?

ELI

Listen, I've already addressed that issue. I have no interest in becoming President. If I ever had to become President, I would appoint a past President like Bill Clinton , George W or Barack Obama as Vice President, I would resign, he would then become President and hopefully, he would re-appoint me as Vice President for the remainder of the term. No 22nd Amendment issue... simple, neat, elegant and effective... insures stability... domestic and foreign.

WAYNE

That's the only reason we're even talking here. A funny thing happens though, when someone becomes President... they don't want to step down... it's this whole ego power thing... we'd need something more formal... something etched in concrete, actually... before we could even consider going with you as Mrs. Plimpton's VP selection.

ELI

Go get me a chisel.

STAFF 1

Wait here.

[*whole staff exits through an adjoining door into the next room, as Eli, alone now realizes Laurie and Jay have indeed been listening in on the conversation and knows this is the moment. He stands up, paces, puts his hands over his mouth, looking out the window,, let's out a whew, and for the very first time, he realizes this whole thing could actually happen... for real... and suddenly the enormity of the position and situation weighs on him... he's nervous, a chill comes over him... but they re-enter and merely thank him and tell him they'll be in touch and escort him out... bummer.*]

CUT TO
[*next day.*]

TV NEWS SHOW:

REPORTER 1
... and in yet another stunner last night, Democratic Presidential nominee Laurie Plimpton announced that she would **NOT** be naming her Vice Presidential nominee until after the Democratic Convention... and would wait up to a week to make that announcement until the last possible moment, fueling speculation of having the first sister and brother in U.S. history as both President and Vice President... and former President... all on the same ticket. How can they do that? The convention has to confirm the nomination for Vice President, don't they?

REPORTER 2
Well, several delegates have confirmed there will be some form of electronic voting next week... each delegate has received a special PIN code and will vote on Plimpton's eventual Vice Presidential nominee by e-mail... *[in a sarcastic tone.]* and hopefully the servers are secure... but it could mean the Democrats are waiting to see how the Republican pre-convention unfolds before possibly... making the decision for Vice President.

REPORTER 3
I think this is the Democrats trying to steal some of the thunder back from the Republicans from Sen. Ruiz's announcement just before the Democratic Convention. It's all just a little theatrical payback.

REPORTER 1
In either case, it is making for one dramatic convention season, the likes of which we haven't seen in almost two generations.

28. Can You Hit a Curve Ball?

BARRETT'S HOTEL SUITE:

[*Emily is there with Dave and camera,
Russ and other aids are milling about.*]

ANN
When is Eli getting here?

RUSS
He's on his way up.

ANN
Good... send him in when he gets here.

ASSISTANT
Sure thing, Governor.

[*Ann exits to an adjoining room and
Emily packs up and begins to leave the
room just as Eli is coming in... they
catch one another's eye, and yes, now
both quite intentionally brush up
against one another through the
doorway giving each other a Cheshire
cat smile and do the brief look back
after going their respective ways.*]

ELI
Ms. Morris.

EMILY
Mr. Eaton.

[*following Emily into the hallway,*
whispering sarcastically.]

DAVE
Good thing that wasn't too obvious!

RUSS
Good afternoon Mr. Eaton. The Governor would like to speak with you, privately.

[*Russ escorts him to the adjoining*
room.]

ELI
Thanks.

CUT TO:

ADJOING ROOM:

[*Ann is pacing and awaiting Eli as he*
enters. She whispers, mouthing...]

ANN
Close the door.

ELI
Who am I to argue.

[*pulling Eli in for a romantic hug.*]

ANN
I've missed you... so much.

ELI
I've been hoping to get you alone in a hotel room.

[*they slowly give each other a kiss and
hold it for a moment.*]

ANN
God knows... I want you.

[*as Eli takes her hand and places it on his...*]

Oh, we are getting frisky, aren't we?

ELI
You've obviously have my... full attention.

ANN
I see that. I can't take this much longer.

[*as they abruptly pull away from each
other, she straightens her jacket and
blouse.*]

ANN [CONT'D]
We've both come a long way. Look at us.

ELI
You've run a brilliant campaign. I'm proud of you.

ANN
I've actually learned a lot from watching you... and I have
been watching you, and I like what I see.

ELI
Damn, Mrs. Robinson, you are trying to seduce me!

ANN
In more ways than one.

ELI
What does that mean?

ANN
Russ has been running the numbers. It looks like Cashman is getting the bulk of Ruiz's delegates and I need to do something... I need a bold move going into the Convention... to show my leadership and to show I'm looking to the future if I'm going to change some delegates' minds.

ELI
Sounds like the right assessment.

[*Eli is now more confident since his meeting with the Plimpton camp and now he's thinking Ann is going to announce him as her choice for VP and is waiting anxiously for the official word to solidify his position.*]

ANN
I'm talking bold.

ELI
Yes?

ANN
I'm talking a family team on the same ticket.

ELI
Laurie and Bill?

ANN
[*short pause*]

Oh grasshopper... I could just eat you up right now!

ELI
[finally getting it...]

I thought I had your number, but you're always one step ahead... I'm guessing most guys are threatened by that... but damn you're good. And I like it.

ANN
Hey, these looks only open up the door. You gotta know how to play the room once you walk in.

[she moves to Eli, pulls him in, they embrace and she whispers in his ear...]

ANN [CONT'D]

Together, we can pull this off...separate, we'll be stale bread in a week. God knows the chemistry is there. You and me...we could turn DC upside down. Screw the Naval Yard... I'm talking the White House... for both of us. What do you say...you and me... married.

CUT TO:

VIEW OF TV :

REPORTER 1
So with Laurie Plimpton's deferral of her Vice Presidential selection, the pressure is mounting on both Governor Cashman and Governor Barrett to reveal their choice for their Vice Presidential choice before the Convention starts up.

REPORTER 2

The Democrats are making a good move here delaying the VP decision. In order to get enough delegates to win the nomination, both Cashman and Barrett need to go public on their choice for Vice President...before it goes to a vote on the convention floor on Wednesday. It's a game of chicken, who will go first... who's going to be the first one to either embrace the public's overwhelming choice... Eli Eaton and set into motion a radical new way that our Vice Presidents will be elected and function in the future, or do you go with a trusted ally... a colleague, or even a brother?

CUT TO:

CASHMAN CAMPAIGN SUITE:

CAMPAIGN MANAGER [STEVEN]

It's time... we've got to make a decision. This can't wait any longer. It makes us look like we can't make the hard decision... and that we're playing games. We need to look Presidential.

STAFF 2
Ruiz is definitely out?

STAFF 3

Yes... He's definitely out for VP, but he'll take State or Defense.

STEVEN
Let's stay focused on the VP

.

STAFF 2
That leaves us with either Eaton... or Barrett.

STEVEN

You're sure she'd take it... if we get the nomination.

STAFF 2

Absolutely... I got first hand confirmation ten minutes ago. She's got the same numbers we have... she knows we've got the lead on this, now.

CUT TO:

PLIMPTON CAMPAIGN SUITE:

STEVEN

Turn on the TV, I've just got word Barrett is going live for an announcement.

ON TV:

TV PUNDIT

In just a moment, Governor Ann Barrett, one of the two remaining candidates for the Republican nomination for President is having a press conference and is about to make an announcement.

TV PUNDIT 2

Our sources tell us she is trailing Governor Cashman in the delegate count... could she be withdrawing and paving the way for a united Republican convention for Governor Jay Cashman?

TV PUNDIT

She could be making an announcement for her choice for Vice President... it may give her an edge going into the voting at the Convention, change some minds.

TV PUNDIT 2

In any case, we'll know momentarily, Governor Barrett is about to speak.

ANN

Good afternoon, everyone. Thank you all for coming. It's been a long campaign... and on the day before our Republican Party begins to vote for its nominee for President of the United States, it is a bright sunny day... so it's appropriate that we look to the future. There are times in our history that mark growth, progress and stability... all for the betterment and advancement of our great country. Should I be fortunate in receiving the support of my party tomorrow, for the first time in our nation's history, it will be virtually guaranteed that we will have come January... our first woman in the White House, as President of the United States.

AUDIENCE

Wild cheering and sign waiving.

ANN

I would like to take this moment to congratulate Laurie Plimpton on receiving her party's nomination for President...

AUDIENCE

A smattering of boos and of polite acknowledgment.

ANN

Please, this is not the time for partisanship

.

[*she starts applauding loudly encouraging others to follow... they slowly do.*]

ANN CONT'D
Thank you.

[Pause]

I am here today to hopefully participate in what should be an historic occasion. I want to be totally transparent with the public. You deserve nothing less. You deserve nothing less from your next President.

AUDIENCE
Cheering, sign waving.

ANN
We have an opportunity to change the way we do business in Washington.

AUDIENCE
Cheering, sign waving.

ANN
Traveling across this great nation of ours, I've heard over and over the frustration people have with the gridlock we have had here in Washington, the bickering, the partisan blocking of the necessary business of our country. We need to restore America's faith in our government.

AUDIENCE
Cheering, sign waving.

ANN
Maybe the solution is to finally have a woman in the White House... as President of the United States!

CUT TO:

BARRETT SPEAKING LIVE:

[live shot of rally from rear, zoom in catching Emily and Dave shooting the event, aside to Emily then close to podium.]

AUDIENCE
Cheering, sign waving.

ANN
... and maybe it's time we have the vision to use common sense, to eliminate special interests from running our country, *[cheering builds up louder and louder.]*   and to lead this country for the benefit of every family in this nation.

AUDIENCE
Cheering, sign waving.

ANN
So today, I am making my personal commitment to that goal... while demonstrating my brand of leadership by being first... making public, my choice for Vice President of the United States of America...   Eli Eaton!

AUDIENCE
Cheering, sign waving. Eaton signs now appear.

[pull back for broad shot, we see Emily pull her headphones off. Eli comes to join Ann, she takes his arm and firmly interlocks it with hers, waving together. Emily is upset as Eli and Ann are hugging each other and look way too personal together.]

ELI

I want to thank Governor Barrett for her courage and the vision...

CUT TO:

29. Pieces to a Puzzle

CASHMAN CAMPAIGN SUITE:

[*TV in the background showing Eli making comments with Ann.*]

CAMPAIGN MANAGER [STEVEN]
That was ballsy.

STAFF 2
Social media is going through the roof. Quote: Very Presidential... A real leader... She's ready for the job...

STAFF 3
Favorables are coming in strong... very strong... very very strong.

STEVEN
That took guts... even though it was a Hail Mary.

STAFF 2
What do we do?

STAFF 3
Time to throw the switch.

STAFF 2
I think she just started a chain reaction... get Jay on the horn. We need to make a decision.
[*holding the cell phone waiting to talk.*]

STEVEN
Hold on a minute... not so fast...the media might be dragging this out for ratings, but we have the same numbers Barrett has... Jay is in... no question. We don't have to make a decision just yet... but get Deep Throat on the line, just in case.

[*add split screen, Laurie Campaign Manager talking on the left side, the Cashman Campaign Manager on the right, both holding cell phones to their ears. They are just standing there staring into space.*]

[an *almost imperceptible nod.*]

LAURIE CAMPAIGN MANAGER [WAYNE]
[*He clears his throat.*]

[*closes his eyes & slight shake of head.*]

CASHMAN CAMPAIGN MANAGER [STEVEN]
OK.

[*without saying another word, after a few moments, both finally push a button and put their cell phones in their pockets and walk away showing empty rooms.*]

CUT TO:
REPUBLICAN CONVENTION:

[*on the large screen TV, voting on the floor, roll call by states shot of Russ, Emily and Dave hanging in a hotel room, part of Ann's suite.*]

DELEGATE AT MICROPHONE IN AUDIENCE
The Great State of Washington yields the floor to our great sister State of Florida.

*[crowd is just seconds away from
erupting in a big bang, confetti, etc.]*

DELGATE AT MICROPHONE
The great Sunshine state of Florida wishes to thank our great sister State of Washington for yielding the floor to us... so that we may cast all of our votes... for our favorite son... and next President of the United States... Governor Jay Cashman!!!!!

*[pandemonium breaks out as Cashman
gets the votes for nomination.]*

[comes in from other room.]

ANN
Guess we just have to wait for the phone call. Russ, tell me I'll be getting a phone call.

RUSS
Jay knows what you want. I trust he knows what's best for the campaign... and the country. He needs you to offset the Laurie effect.

*[Emily develops a sly smile on her
face, knowing that Anne isn't the only
option to neutralize the Laurie effect.]*

EMILY
Do you want any video taken.

ANN
No, I'm too nervous... it will sho

RUSS

Why don't you call Jay now to congratulate him and maybe we can find out what's going on.

[*Ann picks up her cell phone and thumbs a number on the hotel phone...*]

ANN

Hello, Governor Cashman, this is Ann Barrett. Yes, indeed... I just wanted to congratulate you on a great race and I look forward to contributing in the upcoming campaign any way I can... why thank you, I am honored to be considered... sure, if there is any information you need, just give me a call, anytime... I would appreciate that, again... congratulations... sure... good night.

[*listening in on an extension line.*]

RUSS

Nothing really new, but at least you're officially on the short list for VP. We'll know within twenty four hours.

ANN

This is going to be the longest twenty four hours of my life.

RUSS

Why don't the two of you call it a night and check in tomorrow early. I'll call if I hear anything, though.

EMILY

OK... Dave, let's get some dinner.

[*as Emily and Dave leave the room...*]

Emily makes a fist pump in victory,
pulls it down, nearly yelling to herself
in a severely muffled voice so as not to
be heard from the hallway

EMILY
Yes!!!

CUT TO:

[*TV , the next day.*]

REPORTER 1
There you have it. The most dramatic national convention of the last 40 years and the former Governor, Jay Cashman of Florida is the Republican Nominee for President of the United States and will run against Democrat nominee Laurie Plimpton in the race for the White House in November.

REPORTER 2
That's it, the most thrilling convention season in memory. And still...

REPORTER 3
Hold on, hold on...just a moment... I'm getting some information in my earpiece... I've just received an unconfirmed report... make that a confirmed report now, a confirmed report... that apparently both Laurie Plimpton and Jay Cashman have agreed to nominate Eli Eaton as their nominee for Vice President, subject only to being confirmed by their respective party delegates... so for the first time in American history, there will be **NO** race for Vice President... Eli Eaton will be our next Vice President... no matter who wins the White House. We're watching history in the making here!

REPORTER 1

Wow... I am like... totally speechless... all I can say is wow!
Who ever dreamed...

CUT TO:

30. It's Time...

HOTEL BALLROOM:

[*election night party in the ballroom at hotel, the band NRBQ is playing, people are having a great time, it's early on election night and this is Eli Eaton's party, there is no suspense, and definitely no shortage of revelry.*]

CUT TO:
ELI'S HOTEL ROOM:

[*Eli is finishing getting dressed, he's obviously beaming, yet a bit overwhelmed. He's finally able to start up the relationship and the challenge of his life and... it is unknown whether he is going to the reception with Ann or Emily. He moves around the room briefly, looks in the mirror, straightens his tie and proceeds to open the door, the view is from the rear of the room to the hallway door, when immediately, two Secret Service guards are coming in, showing his new found status.*]

SECRET SERVICE AGENT
Its time, Mr. Eaton.

ELI
Please... call me Eli.

SECRET SERVICE AGENT
Sir, as long as you are the Vice President elect of the United States, it will be either Sir, or Mr. Eaton... and at 11:55 AM on January 20th, 2017, it will be Mr. Vice President for the next four years. Whenever you're ready... Sir.

[*Eli, visibly moved by that clear unambiguous mandate, takes a deep breath, pauses then makes a call on his cell phone.*]

ELI

Matt, I'll see you in about a half hour. OK, love you too.

[*he then redials another number.*]

ELI [CONT'D]

Hey you... I'll be there in two minutes... with my posse! Definitely, this is going to take some getting used to, for sure. Oh yeah...I could use a really, really big hug. OK... Bye.

[*as Eli enters the hallway, he looks over his right shoulder and pauses to ponder the setting sun in the window at the end of the hallway and after a moment of reflection, finally turns away, followed by his new entourage... nodding to himself that he's made the right decision.*]

FADE OUT:

THE END

ROLL CREDITS
INSERT BONUS HUMOROUS OUT TAKES AT END OF
CREDITS

para*Flix*®

Would you like to make *The VeeP* into a motion picture? Go ahead... you're the Producer!

Read the brief description of each character on the following pages and then cast the roles with actors [dead or alive] you wish to play these roles in order to bring ***The VeeP*** to life... for your own personal movie production... and hear their voices while you read and imagine the scenes while you experience this...

para*Flix*® DocuDrama

It's a new kind of book.

With **para*Flix*...** It's OK to hear voices!®

* = starring role

Remaining roles are to be played by appropriate people as cameo appearances.

Cast:	Played By:

*1. Eli Eaton: _____

*2. Gov. Ann Barrett: _____

*3. Emily Morris: _____

4. Judge Curtis: _____

5. Arnie: _____

6. Matt: _____

7. Russ: _____

8. Marie: _____

9. Dave: _____

10. John the Elder: _____

11. A.J.: _____

12. Virgie: _____

13. Claire: _____

14. Mr. Jeffers: _____

ST ARRING ROLES

Eli Eaton:

A '40 something' owner of the PIKNIK*S restaurant in Western Massachusetts, down to earth, intelligent, relatively tall at 6' 3", neither especially good looking nor nerdy. Usually well spoken, yet with a direct no nonsense sometimes colorful approach. He is exceptionally logical, an over achiever in life. He always dreamed of making a difference by running for public office one day, and even fantasized about running for national office. Like most people, he got caught up with earning a living and leading a middle class life and raising his son as a single parent after a rather nasty and lengthy custody battle with his ex. He has been a single father for years, and is now looking to fulfill his dream, as his son recently left for college. He, like many others, is fed up with the partisan gridlock in politics today and feels he can set a precedent as an independent bi-partisan VPOTUS and make a real difference.

Gov. Ann Barrett:

A very attractive fortyish ex- high school cheerleader type that every guy in the school wanted a shot at, but never got. Early on, she got caught up in being the driven trophy wife, blondish, perfectly coiffed at the salon, made-up and photogenic... she is an ex Governor of a mid-western state, whose husband was murdered in a convenience store robbery about two years ago. She is very intelligent, conservative, Tea Party and similar to a Sarah Palin type in her passion. She is very driven and is riding the wave of favorable public sentiment following the loss of her husband and witnessing a recent terrorist bombing. She is running for President, but realistically wants to position herself to be the Republican Vice Presidential nominee, [all the media recognition, none of the daily stress]. She hopes to be one of the finalists in the Republican Presidential race, but fears she will ultimately lose out as the Democrats have a female presumptive candidate and the Republican power brokers and donors don't want a guaranteed female President. She usually gets what she wants.

Emily Morris:

An early fortyish, never married type with a slender but non-athletic build and an unassuming low key attractive girl next door appearance. She is an unabashed liberal History magna cum laude graduate from Smith College, who forgoes the spotlight and a high paying career for her principles. She always dresses casually in jeans, or cargo pants/shorts, cotton shirts/jerseys, no make-up, glasses, wears sneakers or sandals, yet a bit more preppie than hippie. Socially reserved, but once engaged, she is extremely opinionated. She's unhappy because she wants to be in the middle of the politics, but had to 'sell out' by taking a videographer job with a Tea Party candidate [Gov. Barrett] in order to pay the rent, and besides, the presumptive Democratic candidate wouldn't hire her. Being very self sufficient, she comes to realize that having a good relationship is necessary for her to fully self-actualize... she can't do it on her own.

SUPPORTING ROLES

Russ: Gov. Barrett's campaign manager who needs to work behind the scene to get Eli out of the picture in order to make room for his candidate.

Judge Curtis: A 60ish local veteran Judge, with an effective and yet down to earth approach to handling things in the courtroom.

Matt: Eli's 19 year old son, just starting college and now finally living away from home, on campus. Matt has been living primarily with Eli since a past custody family court judge awarded Eli sole custody after a long and very bitter custody battle.

Arnie: Eli's 50ish friend and attorney who has to represent Eli at a hearing regarding the viability of his restaurant.

Marie: A small role of Eli's early love interest. She is a youthful 40ish single mother of two teens and is on track to marry Eli and create a newly blended family of five.

John the Elder: A small role of a retired worker at Eli's restaurant who cannot work as much as he wants to because of complex Social Security laws.

A.J.: A small role of a political operative who attempts to get Eli to hire him/her to run his campaign after he gets noticed.

Dave: The cameraman helping Emily shoot footage documenting Gov. Barrett's campaign for President, kind of a work pal.

Virgie: A small role of a Detroit UAW auto worker at a local Ford plant.

Claire: A small role as a voter speaking at a town meeting.

Mr. Jeffers: A limited role of a wheel chair bound defendant in court before Eli's case. He is unkempt, yet is quite articulate with an ironic story.

www.ingramcontent.com/pod-product-compliance
Lightning Source LLC
Chambersburg PA
CBHW070550130626
46556CB00001B/92